Meeting with destiny

Toby Shackleton

Contents

Chapter 1

I t's really hard to concentrate in class on what our teacher, Solayo Ender is lecturing us about. My chair is hard because it's wooden so my backside is becoming quite sore and I feel restless from the storm outside that's brewing even though it's just mild right at the moment and lastly, I'm far from interested in this class. I want it to be over and done with!

"Valerie, can you please sit up straight and pay attention. This will be on the test." Solayo interrupts and then he goes back to dictating straight out of a text-book as he walks around the class, absent mildly, going up down the rows between us, students, especially my friend, Luis and his friend, but not my friend, Kelsey. She's touching his hand every so often, fluttering her eyelids and pursuing her lips, showing off her not over-done makeup and then begins to play with her long, blonde pig-tails that are littered with colourful scrunchies and hair-clips, trying to get his attention.

"What page are we on, Luis?" She flirts. "Uh, 53." He answers, reaching his hand over to turn the page of her text-book for her. Why can't she do it her-self?! It infuriates me and then to really put the point across, her arm that's also littered with scrunchies slips her arm through his to stop him from turning the page. "Kelsey?" He whispers, confused.

I scrunch my hands up, feeling my anger seething. She's all over him, every day, all day long. I wish he was gay so he'd reject her, but he isn't sadly. Infact, every girl in this class likes him. It doesn't make sense! He's not the only male here and... I like him too. How can I even deny it?

His smile, chubby cheeks, piercing, but also dreamy green eyes that compliment his skin, his broad shoulders and fairly athletic frame and lastly, his soft, flyaway blonde hair with brown high-lights is all beautiful. What does he see in Kelsey? What does Kelsey see in him? What does Louis think of every other girl in the class? Most importantly, what does he think of me?

I touch my sides, feeling how much chubbier I am than Kelsey as she's beautifully thin and my wavy, raven hair is not quite at my feet, but it's longer than Kelsey's hair. If Luis had to choose what he prefers, me who's chubby, tall with long wavy raven hair that looks like a birds nest and dark almond eyes that wears all black who's pale as can be or thin, short, lightly tanned Kelsey with her caked-up face and abundance of accessories to go with her pig-tails and all pink fashion sense?

And then I see it, his looking over in my direction right at me. I struggle to compose myself, keep my breathing in sync and thoughts rational and accidentally knock my text-book off my desk which grasps all attention in the room on me. I begin to sink into my chair, wishing I was invisible and feel my sloppy, over-sized cape curl around me, having touched the floor and my pointy hat I'm wearing tilts to the side.

Back a few years ago, apparently the school's uniform used to be different, but it was changed after the fall of this city's former ruler to be less rigid, magic was no longer out-lawed amongst alot of other changes such as Solayo Ender returning to us after a long absence, but I was far too young then to know what was going on and the school here is split into two, allowing for magical studies and Solayo insists we look the part, having told us about fashion of the past, were able to interact with non magical students as not everyone shows potential and we can take off our gowns and hats outside class, allowing the new school uniform to show, but Solayo can be strict and old fashioned sometimes which is fine as his a good teacher and fair alongside honest, kind and caring.

"Valerie Woods?"

I accidentally hit the base of my desk with my knees from jolting suddenly and I see my textbook gently placed onto my desk. Looking up gently from my hands, I see Cloud.

His Solayo's in-class assistant here to support us, but really I know it's because one needs more than one set of eyes on the lookout for a class of 31 students.

"Do you need help?" Cloud whispers as to not disturb the lesson further than I already have, but I scowl, cross my arms and look out to the window. He sighs and heads back over to stand by Solayo's desk.

I can see the faint outline of above the clouds. We used to live in the sky before, there's a city up there, but after the fall of our previous ruler, land was discovered beneath which is where we are now. We can still go up there any time we want, but it's no longer used, just for tours now.

The City has changed alot over time, the nature of what when done, war in a sense. It's taught freely as it's our history, but not everyone talks about it understandably, especially Princess Sophie Golding to this day.

Her own Mum was a tyrant ruler and she kept Sophie a secret for many years. I can't begin to imagine the pain and suffering she went through in secret, but now Sophie's free. It's been 5 years since the day everything changed.

I heard Sophie suffered from poor mental health as a result of her Mum, but also the war. She's getting better and now a young woman who's looked up to at the tender age of 20 by many, including me as she's beautiful amongst many other qualities, but she's hardly ever seen around.

She keeps to a small close-knit circle of friends and spends many hours researching and learning many things, one of the biggest being magic even though her powers burnt out at one point apparently, keeping herself hidden from the public eye in the City's central offices as she still has some challenges to work through, but I do know she spends time outside the office, but it's not on the street unfortunately.

I shift my textbook aside and open my journal an inch to look at the covered pages. I can't imagine what it's like to feel good, not want to die.

Sophie tried to commit suicide many times amongst hurting herself over the years.

Written repeatedly on the pages of my journal is my inner most thoughts which is only one thing:

I want to die.

I can't imagine what it's like to have a family because I'm an orphan, well, a majority of my classmates all know the feeling as the City has orphan numbers, but it's lessening now as were often matched up with family's rather than to be left to langish in a system.

Langish in a system...

That's what my life is like now. It is a system and the odds are always against me. My magic is weak, classes are boring, I have no goals, few friends and no family.

I wonder what it's like to be in love... Well, loved back I mean.

I feel my shoes tapping on the ground lightly and it feels hard to breathe. I pull hard on my cape and cloak to lesson my fabric. It works, but I feel a minor tension headache form. I lower my head to my desk and close my eyes.

"Valerie? Valerie, wake up."

Lifting my head, I see class has finished. "Class has been over since 5 minutes ago." Solayo says, shaking my awake. "I'm awake." I tell him, sniffling and wipe tears with my arm.

He gestures to my cloak, cape and hat. I stand up, remove them and hand them to him. He takes them to the cloak room and returns as I'm packing up my desk.

"Valerie, can we talk?"

"Uh-"

"You've seemed distracted, not focused all lesson. What's on your mind?" He asks, pulling a chair over to sit on, the wrong way, at my desk and I take a seat. "Uh, just other projects and homework I have. School stuff, life, nothing much really. I'm fine." I tell him.

"Oh, yeah?"

"Yes-"

"That's bullshit and you know it young lady. Couldn't be furthest from the truth." And then he places a hand on his mouth, realizing what his done.

"Pardon me and never repeat the bad word I said. But I do want to help, I'm your teacher, Valerie. I can see your anxious, but also feel it. I'm an empath." He tells me.

I nod slowly. "So, tell me. What's really on your mind?"

I shrug and he starts to reach his hand over to my textbook. I realize I left it open. He scans it for just a second, then promptly closes it, laying it back down.

"Valerie, do you understand the gravity of what you've written?"

His caught me out, there's no denying this, talking my way out. "Hmm, you look a little on the thin side." He says, pinching my ribs. I let out a squeal and shove his hand off.

"No, I'm fat!"

"I want to help you." He challenges. "What did you have for breakfast?"

"A handful of grapes..."

"Any water?"

"No..."

"And I can see your hair is brittle. Feels it too." He says, touching a strand, but then lets it go to fall, curling again.

"I'm fine." I tell him again.

"I'm sorry, but I don't believe you and won't be taking your word for it, Valerie. I can see your starving and so, it's no wonder you're feeling unhappy too if you're deprived of adequate dehydration and nutrition. One's body needs fuel so you can function physically and emotionally-"

"Please leave me alone."

"I can't do that, Valerie. I have obligations to you. I'll talk to the King and Queen, we can get you a bed-"

"No!" I shout, shooting straight up to my feet. He stands up slowly as his rather old.

"Valerie, The Hands of Healing Hearts Unit is no longer an Institution where one is placed and the key thrown away. It hasn't been for quite some time.

You have rights, some of which include protection from physical, emotional and sexual abuse from staff and residents. You have the right to food and hygiene, a room with a bed and amenities of your own and there are programs available to you and time outside.

No treatments are not unorthodox or experimental anymore. But medication and some practices can help. There is trained staff, you will be supported.

We can look at what can be done to help you, what's at the centre of why you feel this way." He explains, tapping my book.

"No, I'm not going!" I cry, flinging my arms, but his quicker than me and grasps them. "Now, this isn't up for discussion. You stay here and I'll go see the King & Queen."

"Evil takes many forms!"

I tell him. He looks rather hurt and I see the disappointment in his eyes too.

"Not anymore it doesn't, although I guess it could be said Humanity's far from perfect, but we try alongside doing our best and we'll reach a standard someday. Now, I'm going to get you some help and I'll send Cloud down here to sit here with you, okay? It'll be alright, I promise."

And then he teleports from the classroom, using his powers and I see the door slam shut, a clicking sound and his keys from his desk in a small proof of smoke. I run to the door and press down on the handle, but it's locked and I sink to the floor, back against the door, kneels pulled up and start to cry, letting my tears run free.

Solayo strides down the hallway of City office, his white with green trail robe sliding along the floor after him. He places a hand on his nearly balding aqua blue head and smooths out a few fly away strands. He sighs to himself and heads to turn the corner, bumping head first with someone.

He and the person he ran into doesn't fall over, but they do need to rub foreheads to make the slight pain go away. "Solayo?"

Looking up, Solayo sees it's his friend Cloud he ran into. "Do you think we could talk? If you have time that is." Cloud begs.

"I'm sorry, no. I'm rather pressed for it right now–"

"Please, it'll just take a minute!"

"Cloud, I have a student who's suicidal. I need to report to Zane and Binta."

"Oh..."

"Uh, alright. You have a minute, she's locked in the classroom so I suppose, not much harm can come to her there. What would you want to talk about?"

"Y-you remember my daughter? A-and our friends."

"I do, indeed..."

"Do you think..."

"I'm afraid not, Cloud. I know this is painful friend, but sometimes death happens for a reason. It's inevitable. Just because I have the ability to bend worlds to my will because I'm Kiki & the Core who's the foundation of this world and many others biggest advocate, doesn't mean it's okay for me too. And anyway, it's been far too long now. Had I been around when your daughter passed away from the illness that swept through this city back when June Bendixen was in charge, I could have revived her.

Her soul has been long gone onto another world."

"But I'm her Dad-"

"And you'll see her again one day. We reincarnate a select number of times which is unique to an individual till Kiki judges were done and have learnt everything we needed to learn and experience. There are more souls than we can count and you'll never know when you'll come across one or them again.

Give it time."

"And our friends?"

"Grayson, Mikey and Ester."

"Yes."

"They don't need me this time around, they're okay. There's nothing wrong with helping, but if one's okay, then would it be right for me to interfere morally? I'd end up directing their life and I don't want to do that."

"So why did you let me back in on who you are, allow me to have the knowledge I now know if it's against the rules..."

"There are other rules too and sometimes rules should be broken, but I'd recommend on an informed conversation regarding that with Kiki. And you? You need a friend right now, Cloud.

If I can help, I'm not going to leave you to struggle on your own."

"I just want us and our friends to be a family again."

"And we will be, but not in this timeline and world. Now, can you please go to classroom my friend and sit with the student? It's Valerie Woods. I'll be right back with help, I promise."

"Okay..."

"Thank you friend, now come here. A hug for the road?" Solayo asks, pulling his friend into a hug. "Thank you..." Cloud whispers, trying to fight back tears. "Anytime, friend." Solayo responds, handing Cloud his keys, then they part ways. Cloud to the classroom and Solayo to the King and Queen.

Solayo finds the board meeting office that the city's council often congregants in and gently rasps on the door with his knuckles. "Come in!" A voice calls from the other side of the door.

Solayo pushes open the door to see the room somewhat full. Not everyone is sitting at a long table in the centre of the room though. "Solayo, what brings you here?" Says a voice. "You knocked."

"Ah, Jordan! Yes, hi, I did knock." Solayo responds, greeting Jordan who's a treasurer for a living. They both shake hands and Jordan gestures to the far end of the table. "King, Queen." Solayo bows, addressing the two. They look at him oddly. "Solayo, no offense, Sir, but I'd prefer you didn't call us that. Just say Mayor." The Man responds. "Oh, of course, my apologizes Zane, but it's rather easy to be stuck in the old ways, you know? And two people can really be, 'Mayor' though." Solayo comments.

"I understand, but not all old ways and I don't know what you want me to say, but Mayor is not a dictator and till I think of a replacement word for King & Queen, well, there's two Mayor's." "Zane adds on, shuffling uncomfortably. "Uncle?" The woman next to Zane speaks up. "Uh, yes, Binta?" Solayo answers.

Binta gestures to behind her, pointing over to the large window. A young woman is standing there. "Sophie?" Solayo calls out and the woman looks over her shoulder, hair slightly longer than her shoulder, but not at her feet and loose, but with a plait down the middle of the hair. She turns around the dress she's wearing with boots move every so slightly, tamed by a blue jumper with a round yellow moon on it, featuring the silhouette of a dragon.

She doesn't say anything, but visibly relaxes a little bit. "Still not much of a talker, hey?" Solayo asks, gesturing. "Uh, I wouldn't go as far to say that. She does talks and you know that as before was a ruse, it's just been hard on her now though on her over the years after everything changed... She's better than she was, but I'm not about to push her in a way that it becomes detrimental to her psychological health." Zane tells him.

"Dad?" Sophie whispers, coming over to her Dad's seat and he gently pulls her onto his lap. "Yes, honey?" He responds, eyes cautious and Sophie starts stroking her hand, running her fingers through it. She then looks up. "Go on." Binta smiles gently.

"Can I go out and play?" Sophie asks, tilting her head. "Of course you can! You don't need to ask my permission to do something. Well, provided it's not something dangerous that is." Zane responds.

"Habits..." Sophie whispers. "Old ones..."

"I know." Zane tells her. "Now, where do you think you wanna go?"

"Garden, my friends are out there. And Lillian's out there too!"

"See them outside the window do you?"

"Yes!"

"Well, have fun then. Go on, just you and them all be back for tea-time, alright?"

"Yes!"

And Sophie leaps off his lap, rushing out the door and gives Solayo a small wave on the way out. He waves back, but then he hears two small ouches and Sophie comes stepping back in, but backwards and someone else is with her.

"S-Sorry!" Sophie apologizes, bowing. "What? Oh, no. It's okay, Sophie. I didn't think to knock is all. Don't mind me." A man apologizes.

"Still..." Sophie whispers and the man gently places his hands on the side of her arms. "Where you off too?" He asks.

"G-Garden. I-I want to see my friends." Sophie chokes out. "Oh, cool. You go see them then." The man smiles. "Thank you, Rylan- Ryland. I mean Ryland." She says quickly, stepping around Ryland to leave and he lets go of her, but then she stops and looks back to him.

"Yes?" He says, raising an eyebrow.

"Will..."

"Will I what, Sophie?"

"Come play later with all of us..."

"If you want me too."

"I do."

And then Sophie's gone. Ryland closes the door behind her and then takes a step forward to address the office. He smooths out his pants and blazer and makes sure his badge that's in the shape of a crescent moon is on straight. "Zane?" He smiles.

"How did patrol go?" Zane asks.

"Uh, everyone's good. Not much is going on, city's fairly happy, you know. Just what we'd expect..." Ryland trails off. "You know, all these years before if you had have told me our lives would be very different, but better, I wouldn't have believed you."

"And do you detest it?" Zane enquirers.

"No. I like how my life is now, I'm glad people are happy, especially Sophie.

Our relationship is better, infact my relationship is better with everyone around me! I'm happy here with the way things are!"

"Then I must be doing something right, Rylan."

"And I'm thankful that you allowed me to remain in charge of a force, even if it's not the same one I grew up, commanding- I mean managing."

"Police, not Guards." Zane comments. Ryland nods his head rapidly.

"Now, uh, I've finished my list for the day. Do you have any other jobs for me to carry out?"

"Uh, no. I think were all good here-" Zane begins, but Solayo cuts him off. "Actually, I have something I could use your assistance with if you don't mind helping..."

"Oh? Sure! What is it, Mr Ender?" Ryland responds, turning to face him. Solayo takes a deep breath and then looks around the room.

"There's a student in my class, young girl. Her name is Valerie Woods, in foster care if that's relevant to mention."

"Yes...?" Zane asks, gesturing for Solayo to continue.

"I'm kind of just holding her in the classroom. I sent Cloud to go sit with her."

"Why?" Ryland asks. "Well, I need an escort. I have reason to believe that she's a danger to herself right now." Solayo announces.

"Oh, that's not good. Well, we can certainly do an assessment and talk to Valerie if she wishes to speak with us." Zane murmurs.

"Yeah, so, uh, can I borrow you Ryland just to help transport her down to the Unit? She's a little agitated and doesn't wish to go willingly." Solayo explains.

"Sure, I can help with that. We'll take it slow in bringing her upstairs." Ryland answers. "Go easy, alright? I may allow you all to carry weapons still, but I don't want you using undue force, especially on a child." Zane says, narrowing his eyes.

"Wouldn't dream of it, Sir." Ryland responds, saluting and then he turns to leave with Solayo to head back towards Solayo's classroom.

Binta and Zane share a concerned glance, but then they stand and head over to the window with Jordan, looking out at Zane's daughter, Sophie playing with her brother, Zane's son, Finn and her wife, Lillian and friends, Mia, Ace and Scout.

Ryland is there too and so is Lisa, Mum of one of Sophie's friend, Scout enjoying themselves in the rain that is no longer heavy and turned to a rather light pitter that's great for running around in and splashing in muddy puddles, ruining their clothes.

"Should we go down there?" Binta asks, eyeing her friend, Zane and hubby, Jordan. "Absolutely." Zane responds. "Let's find out where our daughter, Meredith is. Maybe she'll want to play too? Last I knew, she was running around the place." Jordan suggests, taking his wife's hand and they leave the room with their friend, Zane.

I sniffle in the corner, unable to control my tears and repeatedly dry my eyes, wiping snot in the process onto the sleeve of my cloak and cape, point hat titling again.

And then I hear the classroom door creak open an inch, but I don't look up and stay bunched up on the opposite wall to the classroom that's near Solayo's desk. "Valerie Woods?"

"W-what?" I choke out and whoever it is gently closes the door behind them.

"It's me, Cloud. The teachers aide-"

"I know who you are!" I snap and he shuffles his feet along the wooden floor, coming over to me and bends down, a hand placed on my knee.

"Valerie, look at me."

So I do, meeting his eyes. "No one said life was meant to be easy and while I realize you're rather young still, when you're older, you'll understand why suffering exists, but you'll also understand yourself better.

For now though, I want you to know that you can overcome this and even more so with help, Valerie."

I shrug. "Now, do you think you could let me in on what Solayo is worried about, enough that's he'd go to the heads of the city and send me here, asking me watch over a student, you."

I shake my head. "Not feeling too crash hot, ay? That's okay. There will be plenty of time later for us to get to the bottom of this."

And his really starring in deep at my soul. "Cloud, what is it? Why are you starring?" I ask.

"S-sorry!" He apologizes. "It's just... Do you remember me mentioning a few times that I'm... Widowed. Lost my wife and our little girl to the illness that swept through the city a few years ago?"

"Yeah...? We learnt about that."

"Well, today's my little girl's birthday. She'd be around your age today if she was alive."

"What? Really?"

"Yes. Now, Valerie..."

"Why don't we have you taken upstairs now? It's goanna be okay in the long run, you know. There's so much to experience in life. Our own Princess is living proof of that, an example for us to see that. She's alive today."

"I know. Princess Sophie..."

"So, what do you think?"

And then I hear a click and something solid hitting the floor. Looking over to near Solayo's desk, there's a metal brief case with locks on the chair, but it's open when I sware it wasn't a minute ago and I see a ball sitting on the floor, rolling slightly.

"What is that? It looks like it's made out of stone..." I murmur.

"I don't know, but I'd agree..." Cloud responds. Concentrating on it, I feel like it's calling out to me. Saying my name.

"Valerie." Cloud calls, placing his hands on my shoulders to hold me back. "It's speaking to me." I tell him, smiling.

"What? Oh, that doesn't sound good. Valerie, listen, we shouldn't dabble in any private business of Solayo's.

He's a teacher who knows many things, but also an explorer who's witnessed many events first-hand and is more experienced than us."

"It wants me to hold it." I insist, breaking free and reach for it, picking it up in my hands, slowly making my way to stand. Cloud stands up too, right behind me for support. I turn it over in my hands, marvelling at how smooth it actually is in my hands.

"Valerie, listen to me as your student support aide! Place it down right now."

And then I hear the door of the classroom burst open and I see Louis standing there with Kelsey, out of breath. They look up and quickly enter, closing the door behind them.

"The head of the police force is on his way here with Solayo! Valerie, everyone's talking, saying there is a suicidal student. Is it true, it's you isn't it?" Louis enquires, stepping forward to bend down and approach me.

"Valerie-" Kelsey begins. "Can you guys hear it? He can't." I state, showing them the ball and gesturing to Cloud.

"Her what?" Louis asks. "That looks like a Core Control Panel. A few weeks ago, a few juniors went missing. They were playing with it so Solayo started to keep it locked up." Kelsey announces.

"Ah, shit, fuck! Now I know what it is! I forgot about that incident!" Cloud panics.

"Did they ever come back?" I ask. "No." Cloud says, shaking his head. "Where did they go?" I ask.

"Well, according to Core methodology, there are other worlds. They're likely trapped and won't ever come back.

They'll die, lost out there in another world. Weather from old age or a bad entity..." Louis trails off.

Another world... I don't like my life now. I'd be more than happy to trade it in for something else, provided it's better or not, but a stepping stone in my own character growth.

Then why don't you? Take a chance.

I feel the ball say to me and I press on it.

Valerie Woods registered.

Appears on it.

"Valerie, stop, now!" Cloud cries, tackling me and trying to rip the balls from my hands.

Destination selected!

Appears on the ball and I see a circle with an intricate design all over it, appear beneath me and Cloud and it's turning rapidly into a glowing white light that's engulfing the room. Kelsey and Louis step back as they're outside the circle, looking like they're about to run for help.

And then I see them exchange a look, nod and Louis places his hand out and Kelsey grasps it with her hand and they both run straight for us, their capes blowing in the wind that has now entered the room from nowhere, clinging to me and Cloud.

I feel the ball slip from my and Cloud's hands, watching it rolling away, outside the circle and then the room is gone, replaced by darkness and a brief moment of silence.

Then I feel a stone floor beneath my cheek, no longer the wood floor of the classroom and realize I'm lying down. Sitting up slowly, I see a corridor that stretches for a distance to infinite filled with what looks like gateways similar to the star gate we have back home, but not star shaped. Rather, vertical.

"Were no longer home..." I murmur. "Woah, really?! Whatever gave you that idea?!" Snaps a voice beside me. It's Cloud and he helps me up, pulling me to my feet.

"What is this place?" I hear two other voices say and then I see it's Louis and Kelzey, looking all around themselves.

"A gateway between gateways?" Cloud suggests. "Maybe..." I murmur.

"Question now is, how did we get back home? You let go of Solayo's artifact." Louis points out. "Do you think without it, were trapped?" Kelsey suggests.

"I hope not!" Cloud responds. "Why don't we scope this place out? There may be another way out..." Louis speaks up.

"Perhaps. Suppose you're right, we won't know till we try." Cloud answers. "Alright kiddo's, follow me!" He says, gesturing for us all to follow him down the corridor.

We begin to and as I take a step, I feel like the room has just titled slightly, a minor headache forming and my mouth feels dry and I almost fall over, missing my footing all together.

I clutch my stomach. It's been a little over 24 hours since I've really had a proper meal and even some water...

"Valerie, you okay?" Louis calls out to me, holding hands with Kelsey. "Uh, yeah!" I answer.

"Then keep up, I don't want us getting separated from each-other." Cloud snaps and I run to keep up with them while dealing with a now mild burning in my chest and ache in my stomach alongside my other symptoms and we begin to disappear down the hallway together as a newly formed group.

No, family. A Dad and three kids in a weird way...

Chapter 2

I want to stay in this hallway forever if I can and only a small part of me wishes to return home and I know what I've done is incredible selfish. I've trapped three other people here. We don't belong here too and then I see my friends look exhausted, sinking down to sit against a wall.

Come to think of it, I'm tired too. We've not come across much food or water along our travels so we are all at a level of starvation nearly. Day by day, we've all been dropping weight, but I've lost the most. Are we going to die here if we don't find resources or find a way home?

All of a sudden I feel a arm cup my shoulder blade and I turn around wearily. "Valerie, are you okay?"

It's Louis. "Yeah, yeah, I'm fine, Louis, Angel's honour and promise..." I tell him, making a sphere with both my hands.

"You don't look fine, Valerie... You look worse off than all of us, combined. You're deathly pale. Do you feel nauseous, sick or anything?"

"I'm fine Luis, really. I can keep going, we haven't all given up yet so let's continue onwards."

"Really? Cause I feel like giving up and by the way, it's your fault were stuck in this situation." Kelsey wines, crossing her arms, but her complaining goes ignored by Cloud and Luis.

"Valerie, I'm inclined to agree with Luis here. You do indeed look unwell."

Great, now Cloud starting too. "Friends, Team, Family, I'm fine... Really-" but I don't get to finish my sentence as I feel the world start to tilt and I feel a slight pressure on the side of my head like someone's hand is resting on it.

"That was the last of our water."

"It was?"

"Yeah."

"What are we all going to drink now? What am I going to drink?!"

"Woah, woah, woah! Don't be selfish, Kelsey. Valerie fainted, she needs it most right now, more so than you and me."

"That last sip of water may be what just saves her life. Question now is how do we restock our water supply, let alone food reserves?"

"We could go through another gate?"

"Yeah, we could Cloud, but the thing is if we go through another gate that's not habitable to say then we have used energy and it's not expendable at this point, but our efforts would also mean we have come back here with nothing, no food, no water."

"You're right, I shouldn't be hasty. The last portal I led us into resulted in... Nevermind, to unspeakable."

"Oh, don't bring that up ever again as long as we live, I beg you please!" Louis smirks, clinging to Cloud's sleeve and kneeling because his holding me in his arms, hand on my head, propped up on his knee.

"It was guys, it was." Kelsey says snarkily.

I feel a pressure throbbing in my head and let out a raspy breath and use the last of my strength to bring my hand to my head to try and rub my temples, but shortly after my arm drops, a slight thud alerting my friends that I'm awake.

"Oh, shit!"

"Don't sware, Cloud!" Kelsey lectures him.

"Ah, you're right, sorry!"

"Valerie, are you with us?"

It's Luis, but I'm too weak to open my eyes. "Luis... I-I can't open my eyes."

I don't want to tell them about my eating disorder...

"You can't?"

"No..."

"I think two of us should go through a gate while someone stays here with Valerie."

"That's your plan?"

"Well it's not like we have another, Kelsey. Valerie's going to die if we don't do something."

"Can-can you..."

"Valerie, don't try to speak. Conserve your energy." Cloud tells me and then he pulls me up to lean against him more. "Ugh! Come on, fine! Which gate do YOU want to go through, Louis?!" I hear Kelsey grumbling.

"Ummm, let's see... we need to smart about this as we only get one shot at this now and we have to make it count."

"Wait."

"Valerie, do not speak." I hear Cloud lecture me. "My robe..."

"Your robe?" I hear Luis question me. "Get it off." I beg. "She must be too hot in it, these robes are rather thermal." I hear Kelsey say when it dawns on her. "Should I remove it?" I hear Cloud ask. "Just do it, we don't have time for this!" I hear Luis snap say. He's getting really heated now and losing his cool.

I feel my heavy robe removed to reveal my uniform and it's folded up next to my body. "Better?" Cloud asks. I nod weakly, no longer over-heating. "Good, good." I hear Luis say. "Come on, let's just go already!" I hear Kelsey grump and I hear Louis protest, but Kelsey snags his arm and starts dragging him towards a gate.

Some time passes and Cloud places my robe under my head as a pillow, laying me on the ground gently and suggests that maybe I should try and get some rest and he'll watch over me.

After a little while, I open my eyes to see him still patiently sitting with me.

Cloud looks down and sees I'm awake. "Valerie, you're awake?"

"Y-Yeah..."

"We haven't got any more water for you yet. I'm so-so sorry!"

"It's okay... ah!" I whimper, feeling a gnawing in my stomach.

"Don't try to move! I don't want you to accidentally hurt yourself..."

I go to speak, but I don't get a chance as two voices interrupt me and Cloud. "Valerie, Cloud!"

It's Louis and Kelsey shouting. I hear Cloud stand up. "Have we got water?"

"Better!" Kelsey shouts. "Just pick Valerie up! We have to go... now!" I hear Luis add on. I feel Cloud bend down and lift me up bridle style to carry me. I manage to open my eyes and see we are walking along the hallway and come to a entrance, but it's a solid wall just a little inwards.

"Where does this go?" I hear Cloud question. "People!" Louis responds.

"How do you know?" Cloud questions again. "We heard voices and we ducked behind to see a woman with long white hair with aqua blue and light green streaks phase through the wall. That was about 15 minutes ago. We did so we weren't spotted. Let's see if we can break through, we have our powers!" Kelsey tells us.

"It's better than no plan. Surely they would have a doctor or water they can spare for us?" I hear Louis suggest "Alright, let's go then." Cloud responds. Kelsey and Luis take the lead and combine their powers, managing to break the wall instantly that it collapses into pieces we can step over and Cloud follows slowly after them, still carrying me as I weakly clutch my robe.

"We'll get you help, Valerie, don't worry." is the last thing I hear Cloud say before it all goes black again. After some time I open my eyes again to see we are walking along a bridge suspended in the air and there is colours of a sunset all around us. How can the sky be in here with us? Well, whatever this place is... It's beautiful.

The sky is a gentle orange and I see white fluffy clouds float by. It seems to stretch for miles the room. If we can even call it that?

"It's really something huh, Luis?" Kelsey smiles, entwining arms with him.

"Yes. Yes, it is Kelsey."

I can hear them making small talk up ahead. I look to see Cloud is still carrying me. He looks to me. "Are you still doing okay, Valerie?"

"Just... you?"

"Fine!"

"Guys, were here!" I hear my friends scream from up ahead. Cloud hurries up while carrying me and runs a bit faster. He stops behind them and we see a star-gate like the one we have back home, but rather than it lying upright, it's lying flat, suspended in mid-air on it's own and we can't see through it.

"This isn't a normal star-gate..." I hear Louis state.

"Well, are we jumping through, or?" Cloud grumbles. Am I becoming too heavy for him to carry?

My friends take a deep breath in and grasp hands and step forward towards the gate, the tips of their shoes stepping on the edge and we see it light up brightly. White light spills out, blinding us all. I have no choice, but to squeeze my eyes shut while I hear Cloud groan and Kelsey alongside Louis gasp. I wonder what it is they see?

"You four should not be here. You have made a very daft mistake coming here." I hear a female unknown voice say, but whoever she is, sounds only a few years older than us.

"H-hey! What are you doing?!" I hear Louis scream and the next thing I can hear are the screams of Luis and Kelsey together. It sounds like they are getting further away from us.

"And now for you two."

"W-wait! We can talk about this. You see this girl here she's weak and I'm carrying her because-"

"He won't care for your plight, I'm sorry in advance. Although, you do have my sympathies."

And I feel Cloud shift, but he still is holding me. I open my eyes to see a young woman, 25 maybe with dark brown skin covered in freckle with hair a light purple colour in two plaits and she's clutching a head-scarf in her hands and then she shoves Cloud and he slips into the Star-gate with me and the world around us dissolves into light grey with black and white particles and our hair is whipping around, wind running through as we fall and I see the young woman jump in, after us.

"This is not how I planned my week on going, Valerie! I was meant to be taking you upstairs, not downstairs!" I hear Cloud yell right in my ear that my ear rings slightly from it.

Chapter 3

"Then explain to me how were alive!"

Turning my head slightly from lying face down, I see Cloud standing before a man with bright white hair, dressed in purple.

"You're only alive because I want you to be. Step out of line and you will regret making me angry." Says the man, stepping closer to Cloud, getting right up in his face. "No, leave him alone!" I cry, too weak to get up, but reach my arm out slightly and then I feel a pain in my spine, a foot digging in. I let out a scream out of pain and Cloud's faces turns very pale.

"No! Leave her alone, please!" Cloud begs, getting down on his knees instantly, hands clasped together. Tears are streaming down his face.

"If that's what you want." A female voice taunts and I feel the foot on my back removed, but then someone quickly takes a hold of me, turning me over and throwing me onto my back, then presses on a nerve, giving me limited mobility. I see a girl a few years older than me with red and purple toned ombre hair up in a bun, tied of with a black ribbon, but her face is covered by a mask.

One that serial killers wear in horror movies, but hers is fake and it has fake blood on it too, but the blood is almost black rather than red.

"W-who are you?" I choke out. She thinks for a second, then looks me dead in the eyes.

"Just call me, Sherbet, Valerie."

"O-okay, S-Sherbet." I stammer. "C-can you let go of me?"

"Sebastian?" She says out loud and I see the man who was challenging Cloud turn to face us and he signals her. She lets go and stands up straight and now I see it, a shovel strapped to her back.

I weakly manage to clamber my feet, but collapse instantly back on to my stomach.

"Pathetic." Sherbet taunts. "What's wrong with you?" Another voice asks and I see the other young woman from before who pushed us. She has her headscarf now, but her two plaits are visible at the bottom of the scarf, the ends peeking out.

"Why did you push us?!" I snap. "I had no choice." She responds. "I hate you!" I tell her.

She looks sad and nods her head. "I don't blame you..." She whispers, turning to walk away like a dog with it's tail between it's leg and then I see a young man with dark brown skin and normal raven hair walk up and he places his hand on her shoulder.

"Get some rest, Harriet. You've been up all night. We'll take it from here."

"Thank you, Owen..." She whispers, then leaving and I see another woman who's pale with long white hair with green and blue streaks that's pushed over to hang down one side of her face that's almost as long as my hair. "Who do we have, hubby?" She speaks up. Owen looks panic stricken and slides a few cm away from this woman. "Three minors, two girls, one boy and an adult male." The man near Cloud answers.

"Oh, that won't do at all. Especially not for not challenges, experiments and work." The woman says, huffing a strand of loose hair out of her face.

"Wait, what?" Cloud gasps. "Cloud, who are these people?!" I beg. "Be nice to my parents." Sherbet hisses. "Parents?!" I respond.

"Something like that, yes. Shelby here, I and Harriet owe our lives here to Sebastian and Rain... I'm Owen." The man near Rain who's just introduced himself.

"Oh, thanks for ruining the suspense & mystery." Sherbet growls, pulling the mask off her face and stomping away.

Owen looks worried. "Oh, she'll be fine." Rain says to him. "Where are our friends?!" I cry, looking to Cloud.

"I don't know! These psychos took them away. They have a security team here. I refused to leave you as you were unconscious. You brought me time!" Cloud tells me.

"Where do you take Louis and Kelsey?!" I cry, glaring daggers at Sebastian, Rain and Owen. "They're in lock-up at the moment. Would you like to see them?" Sebastian answers.

"Valerie, do not trust them!" Cloud begs and I see Sebastian very quickly hit him across the back of the head with a blunt object, knocking him out. "Cloud!" I cry, struggling to move.

"What is wrong with you?" Rain snaps. "I have anorexia!" I shout. "We've been stuck in a gateway between gateways the past three days!"

"Alright, we can work with that." Sebastian says. "What?" I ask and Rain approaches me, gripping my chin to look her in the eyes. Her hands are ice cold. "But just so you know, Valerie... This is our world you've stumbled into. While your here, you will obey all orders otherwise we'll see you what were really capable of." She hisses.

"Capable of?" I wonder and I see her eyes turn from a blue to a cherry red colour and so does Sebastian, but from brown to purple when his was caramel brown a moment ago.

I look to Owen who shrugs, hands in the pocket of a green sweater. "Do as they wish, Valerie." He says. "What, why?!" I cry out.

"Harriet, Shelby and I are human unlike them." And then he shuffles away quickly.

"You're like us?" I ask, face still in Rain's hand. "We already knew based on your clothing. They're Solayo's uniforms." She retorts.

"You know him?!"

"More, know of him. We don't bother with him, Valerie. His James and Julius's problem, not ours. We prefer humans as they're far less complicated and more straight forward, but no one said sophistication wasn't any fun."

"What? And who's James & Julius-" I begin, but then she lets go of my chin and snatches the collar of my shirt and begins to drag me across the ground forcefully behind her that I gag and choke a bit.

I see Sebastian claps his hands together and the terrain around us turns from a bright, grassy green to all out, white snow and ice, dark colours clouds beginning to roll in, within a matter of seconds and I see him lift Cloud up in his arms, following Rain.

Am I alive? Am I dead? Looking around me, I see nothing, can smell nothing.

Where am I? And then I feel like I'm being sucked up a straw as if I'm liquid. It's a weird feeling and I quickly squeeze my eyes shut. When I open them, I see the dim blueness of a room and and I'm lying on a bed, the mattress stripped bare of sheets and a pillow.

There is an IV pole nearby and it's empty. Climbing off the bed slowly, feeling my body ache like I've never felt before, I walk around to the end of the bed and see a space for where a chart would be, but it's missing and I see a curtain next to me. Slowly, pulling the curtain back, I see another bed that has sheets and a pillow, but it's also terribly messy and lying on the tile floor is a small pile of crisp white, but clearly used bandages. Why would they be laying here?

And then I hear the clock on the wall behind me start ticking. Turning around, I see the hands are set to 1:01 a.m.

What happened here? And then I feel a stabbing pain in my chest, collapse and the feeling of being sucked up a straw comes back and I squeeze my eyes shut again.

"Valerie, Valerie! Wake up, please!"

My eyes open suddenly and I feel myself thrown forward, gasping for air. I'm sitting on another bed, but it looks more like a doctors examination bed and I'm drenched in sweat, my clothes not my school uniform.

"Do you think it was a nightmare, Luis?"

Turning my head because I feel delicate hands on my shoulders, it's Luis and he looks...Different? No, older. I look beside him and there is Kelsey, but she looks different too.

"Louis, Kelsey?" I whisper, seeing they're wearing the same light grey pants, t-shirt and socks as me. "Yes, it's us!" Kelsey beams, jumping excitedly.

"What happened?" I ask. "Where are we?"

"You were screaming in your sleep. Nightmare?" Luis probes. I wipe sweat from my forehead, then answer him. "I don't know." I tell him.

"Now tell me what happened." I beg, hopping down off the bed, but stagger and Luis and Kelsey both take hold of either side of me to steady me.

"Valerie... We don't know much more than you. We woke up on similar beds." Kelsey points out. "And we look older like we've aged... I don't know how or why, but we are." Louis says and we all inch towards a large, tall mirror attached to the wall.

They're right. We look as if we're around 18-20 old at-least. I don't know, some number in our 20's. We stare at our reflections for the longest time and slowly, Kelsey's hand grips my shoulder and Louis places a hand on my back.

"Guys?"

We all flinch when we hear a voice and turn our heads to see the door of the room is open and Owen from before is standing there. He enters the room and our jaws drop, seeing Sebastian follow him in.

"What did you do us?" Louis snarls. "What do you want from us?"

And he slides an arm around me and Kelsey, holding us close to his body.

Sebastian chuckles and shakes his head. "Humans are simper than magical beings. Magic is sophisticated and while power is fun and great, I don't like great difficulties.

We rarely have new people come along and because of that, I have a lack of people to test on or play with or put to work for me.

You guys and your adult friend will be staying here and till I decide what purpose you will fulfil or role, try to make yourselves useful. Too many people naturally means a lack of resources."

And then he turns to leave, but looks over his shoulder, smirking. "And by the way? I aged you guys up to adults."

And then he leaves. Owen looks at, seemingly nervous, then quickly hurries away, following Sebastian.

A man and woman we haven't met before, turn the corner. "Um, hey? I'm... Ricky and this is Paige. Were this community's guards. Well, two of them anyway. We've been tasked with giving you guys lodging, but all that's left is a shared boarding house.

Hope you don't mind and please follow us." Ricky asks. We begin to follow tentatively.

"R-Ricky?" Luis stammers. "What?" He snaps. "Will we be seeing our mentor again?" Louis worries.

"Soon, folks. His waiting for you." Paige responds.

Chapter 4

The world around us was a dense woods before, but now it's covered by a thick blanket of snow. We've all seen snow before, but back home on the ground, it hardly snows anymore. It just doesn't reach us unlike what it did when we were stuck trapped in the sky before.

I wonder if it's possible to have some fun while were here? Would sure upset the leaders here if we did.

"Guys!"

I look up to see Cloud standing in-front of what looks like a boarding house. We all start running towards Cloud and he embraces us all in a hug, but then pulls back. Ricky and Paige smile to each-other and walk away.

"Guys, listen to me, this situation is really bad, I'm not goanna lie to you and Valerie don't blame yourself, okay? They have everyone here, normal people like us are being held prisoner here, they're not free to leave and being forced to work long hours in a variety of positions all for the sake of 'earning their keep' to live here.

"I will admit this all very suspicious situation, Cloud. I suspect there is more going on than just what meets the eye. These people have altered us, Cloud. Look, we look like adults!" Cloud panics.

"Oh, you guys, do..." Cloud stammers, clearly worried. "Do you remember what they did to you?"

"No sadly." Louis and Kelsey respond, saying the exact same sentence. I think back to waking up. My dream... I really don't want to talk about it, it was just a nightmare, I bet because of whatever was done to us. A side-effect of it.

"Uh, so... What do you guys want to do? I have a suggestion, but I'm not going to force you to anything you don't want to do and, you may look like adults and the psycho leaders here may want to treat you like adults from here on out, but I want you to know that you guys aren't adults, okay?"

"B-but we are..." Kelsey whispers. "No, this is just on the outside you hear me?" Cloud growls. "You're not listening."

"Hey! Instead of arguing about this, can we talk of escaping?" Luis demands and looks to me. I look back at him. "What you want to me to back you up?" I ask. I see Kelsey glare at him, saying, 'this is your fault were here'

She's two faced, I know she is. Will act like she loves everyone around her and want to be their friend, especially in-front of Louis, but I know what you're really like when his not around. I cross my arms.

"We should leave... So, how you guys wanna do it? We fell down through a portal." I speak. "It might be possible to go back up the way we came." Cloud smiles, reaching out to touch my shoulder.

"Not sure, but we will find a way in the end hopefully. I believe in us!" Kelsey smiles, squinting her eyes and wavy pigtails filled with sparkly clips, held by colourful scrunchies bouncing with her as she moves around.

"So, if we are stuck here for the moment then... what do you suggest we do in the mean time?" Kelsey snaps all of a sudden, her fake-good mood changing. "Do what everyone else is doing?" Louis suggests while pointing. Me and my friends turn around to see other people are talking in small groups, a couple handshakes or something is exchanged. People are exercising and some are taking a breather with equipment like gardening tools set up, dug into the ground next to them.

"We can pretend to blend in for the moment, but getting out of here will be our primary focus." I whisper and then a chill runs through me and my friends. We all shiver. "It's cold here." Luis mumbles. "We should head to sleep or something for tonight. It's becoming dark out soon, not to mention cold and still exhausted from being lost for days.

If we are somewhat rested we can come up with a plan in the morning for escaping, but we have to be smart about this, because if those people running this place find out? I would hate to think what they will do to us!" Cloud worries. We all nod.

I end up shivering again. "Aww, poor thing." I hear Luis say and he comes over to give me a hug to warm me up. I see Kelsey look subtly angry.

"I wish I had my robe from class now." I mumble. "Me too." Kelsey states and then she looks to Cloud. "They confiscated all our clothes, I.D, anything we had on us."

"Well, shit. This makes things hard now doesn't it? Not to mention, we'll be dependent on this community for the things we need." Cloud curses. The lights around us begin to dim and I see people heading into the large building behind us, the world around becoming much darker.

"Everyone get to your sleeping quarters, it's lights out!" A guard calls. I jump back a bit scared and Kelsey grasps onto me, twitching nervously slightly. Once everyone is gone, it's just me and my friends. "Did you not hear what we said?!" The Guard grumps at us. "We would, but we don't know where WE are sleeping!" Kelsey bites back.

"I could write you up, ha!" Grumps the Guard. "Go through those doors and you along with your group are in the last room on the left at the end of the hall. In other words... Now, go!"

The Guard walks away from us and we decide it's best just to head inside. Get out of this snow for a start.

After we have located our room are settled in, we each start poking around. We conclude were safe 'as such' but people could still be listening, everywhere."We need to find somewhere to talk freely." I whisper. "What, why?" Luis asks. "She has a point though." Cloud speaks up.

"People in this place could be looking out for themselves and likely wouldn't hesitate to throw a friend under the bus or double cross someone."

"Anyway..." Kelsey announces. She walks over to two cupboards in the room and opens them revealing... Grey P.j's and clothes that are also grey like what were wearing now. "I like colour, especially pink." Kelsey pouts. "The clothing every else is boring too. Browns, dark yellows, dark green and mostly grey and other colours that are clearly faded and everything."

"Other than the clothes here, Kelsey which you're complaining about, the room it's self is small. Four beds and a balcony we can go on and that's it. My guess is bathrooms are located somewhere else and it's a shared one." Luis states, placing a hand on Kelsey's back who smiles at him, tilting her head.

We all end up changing into the P.j's provided and each claim a bed. We all wish each-other and bunker down to sleep for the rest of the night, wanting it to pass quickly so we can form an escape plan and get it into action asap.

Chapter 5

I don't dare entertain the idea of what the punishment is for refusing as the security and leaders mean business. "Valerie, you ready?

I hear Louis call my name and I push my thoughts aside to see him holding the door to our room open, Kelsey and Cloud already outside of it, looking in. Louis extends his hand to me and I take it, rushing out of the room, following him.

Security leads us and a few other groups out of the dormitory to a cafeteria of some kind. We choose a table somewhere in the fray and take a seat "Roll call is in beginning in 5 minutes and then breakfast will served!" We hear Ricky announce to the room. "You... okay?" I hear Kelsey ask me, cautiously.

I say nothing. "We've had a couple of rough days, Kelsey. Valerie's still recovering." Louis objects. "Maybe she just needs a really good feed and a drink of water and will feel like her old self in no time." Cloud suggests. adds on. He wants to come up with a solution and I thank him for it, but I really am not looking forward eating and drinking...

Names have started being called and

all of a sudden, I feel a cold hand grasp my shoulder and pull me to my feet. My eyes meet a pair of cherry pink eyes with long white hair in a ponytail framing her face like it did yesterday who's just like us, but me, Louis & Kelsey are still too young or haven't really come into our powers and develop the unique eye colors and same goes for our hair.

I hear Ricky stop reading and everyone gasp. It's Rain and she trails a hand across the back of my neck causing me to shiver. Her skin feels like it's almost ice cold.

I see her smirk and she turns and walks away from me, her mission ti likely scare me, accomplished. I look to see her stand by Sebastian who is also accompanied by Owen and Harriet.

"You're not very attentive, Sprout. Keep that up and you'll soon learn what's reserved for slackers. We don't like slack-ers." I grit my teeth upon hearing Sebastian's remark. "Awww, don't be so tense, Sweetheart. There's no need." Rain says in a cutesy tone. This only makes me feel angrier.

"Wait!" A voice calls out and I see Cloud leap to his feet. "Uh, yes?" Sebastian responds.

"I recognize you guys! All four of you! You're from the world we came from. Why are you here and still look how you did before?"

"Not playing games, I see." Sebastian jokes. "Were far more experienced angel's than you guys. Every world is different, but every outcome also has other possible outcomes.

And were not like you guys too. Rain & I here remember every world we pass through and were not in the business of forgetting unlike other people. Also, if their is a timeline we particularly enjoyed in the past, we see no problem in replicating events to a certain extent."

"You mean people too." Cloud snaps, pointing a finger directly at Harriet. "You. You were one of June's Bendixen's maids and later took off. I never found out what became of you.

You were alive, but didn't want to talk to me. You were my girlfriend, Harriet." Cloud says with a tear streaming down his face. My ex died and so did my daughter. I was lucky I could find love again after the plague that swept through the city of where I came from."

"I don't know you..." Harriet whispers, looking distressed between Rain & Sebastian. "Even if there is a past, guys, re-living it may not be important. I and Harriet trust in Rain and Sebastian here. Were Human compared to them and they won't lie to us or hurt us.

Everyone here including us knows what they are and they're intentions aren't intended to be bad. They want the best for us at the end of the day." Owen speaks up.

"I don't believe that for a second! What bull-crap!" Cloud challenges. "You aged my students and are forcing us to stay here."

"Word of advice, Cloud..." Sebastian trails off. "Compare the evils. Were the lesser of the few."

"What's that supposed to mean?" Cloud growls.

Rain shrugs. "We don't interfere with them, they leave us alone. It's sort of an unspoken alliance and mutually beneficial for all of us."

"I don't have time for this." Cloud snaps. "I want proper answers and I know you and your wife have the ability to send us back from where we came!

And Harriet..."

Harriet looks at us blankly and then I see a sparkle in her eyes deep below. "Cloud?" She says, tilting her head and is about to step forward when Rain seizes her shoulders and Harriet's dark skin and dyed purple hair which she clearly did to mimic Rain & Sebastian's status turn blue, almost like ice.

A cloud of air comes from Harriet's lips. She's shivering and crying. "Rain!" Owen panics, but Sebastian puts an arm up, stopping here.

"What are you?" Rain hisses. "S-sorry..." Harriet murmurs. "I can't hear you, speak up." Rain huffs.

"I-I'm, s-sorry." Harriet tries again despite Rain literally freezing her to death. I see she wields Ice. I wield Ice. Well, did. Past tense.

"For?" Rain asks.

"For d-disobeying you, I-I'll be better, p-please Rain..." Harriet chokes out. "Good enough." Rain says, letting go of Harriet who wraps her arms around herself.

"Paige, be a sweetie and take Harriet up to the Hospital. Have London warm her up." Rain demands and we see Paige who helped escort us last night remove Harriet from the building.

"You people are okay with this?!" Cloud yells, looking at the other table and we see a young woman with dark brunette hair in pigtails stand.

"No, but they're the leaders and mean well sometimes. And for the record? We don't like magic. They told us about you guys last night and said they stripped you guys of yours. The young adults with you look inexperienced and would do so much worse than Rain and Sebastian we think. And you? Aren't even magic at all.

I can see your young friends still have small features to show what they used to be unlike you who is clearly human. Now, here on out, do this community a favour and don't drag us down with you."

Then she sits down. Everyone in the room says something along the lines of agreeing with her or showing it by clapping.

Cloud looks scared and quickly lowers himself to resume his seat.

"Now, with intrusions and defiance out of the way..." Sebastian says. "Any of you who don't have work to go off too, please remain here after breakfast and work will be assigned to you.

The ones who do, you know what to do."

And then breakfast commences. Sebastian with Rain followed by Owen who is standing back, walks up to us.

"How are you guys holding up with the winter weather?" Sebastian chuckles. I look at my friends and I see now Louis is holding Kelsey in his arms. The look of fear in both their eyes are scary. Cloud shrugs. "It doesn't bother me, I've encountered worse."

"Oh, have you now?" Sebastian laughs.

"Cheer up, sweethearts. This is your home now. Live by our rules and I think we'll get along just fine." Rain adds on in a cutesy voice again. She walks up to me and I feel her give the side of my face a slight tap with her hand. Her hand is really cold from powers, but maybe suffers from a medical condition on the side too?

She's pale as can be which is odd as Angel's should have glowing skin...

"Maybe you all need a lesson to be taught your places anyway just so we know were all on the same page for the future, hmm?" Sebastian smirks and we hear a voice interrupt.

"No! Uh- you- you don't have to do that!"

Looking, we see the young woman who just threatened us is now coming to our defense. "Samantha." Rain speaks, eyes narrowing.

"I beg of you, just leave them alone, please. We were all new at one time or another and you always show us mercy till we learn our place." Samantha adds on.

"True, but what if we don't feel like it this time?" Sebastian smirks.

"Be the bigger person, please." Samantha tries again.

Sebastian and Rain start whispering between each-other, then turn to face us all again. "We have an idea, you lot. Learning to work a job is difficult when you're starting out and you and your kiddo's, Cloud may not be ready for it, but till that day, why don't we see if we can get you on he road to succession.

You earn your keep here like any person who runs a community would expect, but why don't we have some fun? We plan events, parties per say from time to time to boost morale so let's have something along the lines of our own... Fun-run per-say. It'll help you train up anyway to carry out working long hours on our farm or something.

Yes, I like the sound of this for the mean time." Sebastian says, smiling wider and wider.

"W-what..." Kelsey stammers.

"Enjoy, guys, this is all for you. Use it as a stepping done to greater things. Our security will be in touch with our further instructions so please do await them." Sebastian adds on, then him and Rain turn to leave, but Sebastian looks over his shoulder.

"Welcome to Destiny."

Then he starts to laugh. "Destiny?" Kelsey asks confused. "I'm not sure weather us fulfilling the games they're playing is what they mean by 'Destiny' or it's this community's literal name..." Louis speaks up, reaching for Kelsey's hand.

"Samantha?" Cloud whispers and we see her shove him right to the ground, his knee becoming grazed because the fabric of his pants tore open. Samantha's fists are clenched and her teeth gritted. "Cute. Just cute, all of you. Particularly you, Cloud. Did I not just warn you?" She snaps.

"Warn us? This is your fault-" But she doesn't let Cloud finish and promptly punches him in the stomach. He winces. "Watch it, I'm becoming your elder."

"Someone's your ally and then your friend a moment later but next thing you know, they're also your rival and are the one holding a knife through your back." Samantha says, kicking Cloud in the ribs. "Learn your places, the leaders here aren't truly forgiving.

They only want you to think that, entice you into liking them and when they have you wrapped around their finger as their servant if you stop being their toy, you're disposed of.

Believe me, we've seen it."

And then she's gone as she came. We panic and all rush to help Cloud up who tries to tell us his okay, but it's clear his not okay.

"Samantha, you're rations will be cut for today!" We hear a security call out, going after Samantha. "Oof." Louis comments. "Double oof, I think." Kelsey adds on and while Security is distracted, we see a girl with dusty hair, held in place by a black, frilly headband sneak around them, poking her head up at the back of table, snags a stick of jerky and a bottle of water and is gone, heading the same way Samantha went.

"Either alot of people here are hungry which is a common punishment or she's stealing that for Samantha. Her and two guys were hanging back when Samantha was bullying us, yet challenging authority. I think they're her friends.

"Jobs are commencing in 20 minutes and new group, we'll be debriefing with you in 20 minutes also!" We hear Ricky from Security call out. "Ah, let's just eat..." Cloud winces, hobbling over toward an obvious line of people who are awaiting food, rejecting Kelsey and Louis's attempts to support him and I trudge slowly behind them, feeling weak. I'm hungry and there's food there and I need some energy so I don't faint on my friends, but everything inside of me is telling me to find a way to hide my condition no matter what.

Chapter 6

Looking up, I see the young woman who stole before and she gives me a small wave. 'What's your name?' I signal. 'Avery' she mouths back to me and then I see her stumble slightly, but she regains her balance.

Looking at everyone who's out here with us, as a few more than just us were rounded up for "fun"

Everyone is clearly starving to some degree, but Avery appears to be the strongest of them all. Okay, not the strongest, but she's doing far better than everyone else.

Clearly, she hasn't been punished much.

"12 minute break everyone!" I hear one of the security guards call out. I flop onto the snow with my friends, just letting go.

"My insides are burning!" Kelsey whinges. "Mine too!" Louis follows. I see Cloud and his just trying not to say anything, but I can tell he is in a smidge of pain.

"Water available!" I hear one of the Guards yell. I see the look on Kelsey and Louis alongside Cloud's face when they hear those magic words. They are up and joining others to get water. I heave myself up slowly when I feel a hand grasp mine and I'm pulled to my feet.

"I won't be giving you special treatment." I hear a voice snap. Turning around, I see it's Shelby. "Why-" I begin. "And Owen likes you." She says. "Does he?" I ask. She shrugs. "You aren't the first and you won't be the last. He started with Harriet, then Dana and now you."

"Who's Dana?" I ask, but she just glares at me. "You're exactly like Dana in almost every way. You're pathetic and a weakling. I can see it now, you'll be dragging people down just like she did. I've let Ricky and the others know not to give you any water. Let's see how long it takes for your condition to truly worsen and your body gives out too."

"You can't do that! That's torture."

"Oh, so it's okay to punish yourself, but I'm not allowed too?"

"W-what, no!"

"Then act normal, you freak."

"You're a psycho wearing that serial killer mask you had on, and I can't just act a normal! This is-"

"But she press her fingers against my lips. "Nah-ah, I don't want to hear it. Take this moment without water to reconsider your choices because I guarantee you my parents and brother may have said their fine with your condition, but they're actually not.

Good luck, I bet you won't last till mid-day till you're begging for some water and maybe even food."

"Is that a challenge?"

"View it however you want, Valerie, I don't care."

And she walks off. I shake my head and heave myself into the water line. I don't want to die exactly... I'll see if I can bargain with the Guards. When I make it to the front of the queue, muttering under my breath how much Shelby is a bully, I plead with the Guard, giving him puppy eyes because there is one bottle left and she says nothing, just stares at me so I reach for the last bottle only for her to smack my hand way.

She smirks and cocks her head to the side. "Fuck you." I hiss.

She flicks her fringe and shakes her head, then gestures for me to move away so I begin to leave. "And Valerie?" She calls out. "What?" I ask.

"We'll see about... hmm, afternoon tea time maybe? If you last that long." She snickers. "Or you can tell on me and Sherbert to Sebastian and Rain, but do know, if their is one thing they don't like, it's snitches." And she takes the bottle for herself, drinking it and goes off in the other direction. I turn around and prepare to head towards my friends when I cross paths with Samantha's group and Avery look me dead in the eyes. Them and the others, two guys are leaning against a wall. The guys are sharing their water with Samantha while Avery has her own.

Avery goes to step forward, but Samantha takes hold of her shoulder. "Remember who's your cousin and team leader." She says cruelly.

The look on Avery's face says it all. "It's okay, thanks anyway." I mouth to her. No doubt she feels bad though. I head onwards back to my team. They all have water.

"Drunk yours already?" Louis questions. I see his half way through his bottle and Kelsey alongside Cloud are sculling theirs. "They ran out..." I mumble quietly. Kelsey immediately stops gulping and passes her bottle to me without hesitation.

"Wow, that is just sitting on cruel." Cloud snaps. "They could have brought more supplies out."

"It's fine, really." I respond. "Valerie, have what's left of mine. Without it, you will faint... or worse." Kelsey says. Do they know? I push the thought aside and accept what's left.

When I'm done I hand the bottle back to Kelsey. "Oh, hey, look..." Louis says. I turn around and see Rain standing in an enclosed watch tower above. I see her shake her head and she turns around and says something to someone, but I can't make it out. I see Harriet come into view though and nod her head at what Rain said.

"You know usually they would have just locked you straight up for not abiding by anyone's command. You're lucky they're letting it slide." I hear a familiar voice. It's Samantha with her team behind her. "Command, sorry, what? We've done nothing to them." Kelsey growls.

"Oh, nothing." Samantha taunts. "Shelby tried to bully Valerie!" Avery speaks up suddenly. "Avery!" Samantha hisses. Hey, that's not fair to deprive her of water!" Kelsey shouts.

"Fair or not, this could have been worse for you. They could have locked her up."

"Worse, how?!" I see Kelsey yell again, throwing her arms up, becoming annoyed. "I just said, locked her up."

"And what do you mean by that exactly?" Louis questions.

I see Samantha flinch and she look scared. "They've done it to you haven't they?" Clouds calls her out on. I hear her groan. "Solitary confinement. If they don't feel you're obeying them, they teach you a lesson. You wouldn't have liked it, very cold." She finally answers.

"That's it? Okay, yes that sucks, but they would have let her out, yeah?" Kelsey asks. Samantha shrugs. "Depends on Rain and Sebastian's moods. They call the shots around here, not actually Owen, Harriet and Shelby. Might have been the whole day, but let out at dinner. Who knows really? Rain not coming down here is you getting off luckily."

Cloud scoffs at her statement. "It's very dark too!" Avery quickly adds on, but Samantha quickly shushes her. "Back to training!" I hear a Guard call out and Samantha quickly walks away, followed by her team. As we are preparing to head back to training, Avery looks back to me and mouths "Lunch" to me, then nods her head.

It's now lunchtime and everyone has returned the cafeteria after more strength training exercises. I feel knackered and I'm on my own. It's so unlike my friends to just ditch me. Where are they? I'm distracted from my thoughts though as a dead weight bumps into me and knocks me to the ground. "Oh, sorry."

It's Avery. She has a small grin and presses something into my palm. It's a super small energy bar of some sort. "You have only till afternoon tea time now, I heard the Guards say they're going to let you suffer a little longer. It'll come soon, don't worry." I hear whisper, then she picks herself up and heads to the food line, taking a tray of food. I hide the small bar between my hands that it can't been seen.

I hear one of the Guards tease Avery from afar that's she's clumsy. I stand up slowly. I need to find somewhere I can eat this without being seen or no doubt, it will be taken away from me. I leave the Cafeteria without issue and head down a side street of the city. Luckily no one has seen me when I feel a hand reach for mine and I'm pulled into somewhere. It's dark.

"Who-who's there?" I stammer, tearing up. I see the space around me, light up. It's Kelsey and she's holding a lantern. "Come, Cloud's so clever." and she leads me. Eventually she pushes a brick into the wall and a door opens. We go in. I end up in a room resembling a study, combined observatory. Cloud is on a platform, looking through a telescope and Louis is at a book shelf, reading a book with a note-pad sitting on-top and a pencil in his hand.

Kelsey places the lantern near Cloud. "Got her. I thought I was goanna have to go onto the streets, but seems someone snuck away."

"Where are we?" I ask. "I have never seen a star constellation system quite like this before..." I hear Cloud trail off. "No idea where we are." Kelsey rolls her eyes and Louis turns around to face me and Kelsey. "Like it?"

"What is this?" I ask.

"Hidden room that seems to have been boarded up and locked. If you look under the central table, you can see a love heart scratched underneath. Says: 'Dana' inside." Louis responds. "I think it's safe for us to talk in here."

"Cool, huh?" Kelsey adds on. I nod. "You okay?" She asks me. I see a chair near the table and take it. I pull out the energy bar to discover it's infact a candy bar and tear the wrapper off. "They feed you?" Louis questions. I shake my head. "Avery pulling more wool over eyes." I respond and start scoffing the bar.

When I'm done, Kelsey takes the wrapper. "We'll get out of this place, Valerie. I promise you, you don't belong here, don't deserve to be stuck here just because you made one bad decision based on poor judgement."

I nod. "You want a nap? You look like you need it." Louis questions, pointing to a nearby couch which has a light grey scarf with silver stars hanging over the back. "Are we done for today?" I ask. "Yeah, afternoon free now. We passed Harriet in the street and she told us Rain said everyone's working hours, well, our training hours in retrospect has been ended early. Take a nap." Cloud speaks up, interrupting, but not pulling away from looking at the sky.

I walk over the the couch and Kelsey helps me to lay down. She grasps the scarf and folds into a small pillow and slips it behind my head. "There is an old coat in the cupboard that's indigo colors with rain clouds and umbrella's on it. Give that to her as a blanket." Louis smiles, gesturing to a small cupboard. She finds the coat and brings it over to me for a blanket, then plonks her butt down next to me. "Just goanna rest my eyes and body a minute. I feel kind of nauseous..." she mumbles. "Uh-huh." I hear Cloud state, not listening to hard while Louis looks sad, but goes back to reading and writing something on his note-pad. I yawn and start to drift off similar to Kelsey.

"Oooh - the big and little dipper!"

"Cloud!" Her and me shout at him while Louis shouts at him also for waking both us, girls.

After having a nap, I head back to the city center with my friends as they wanted some time to think about the mysterious room. It's cool we have a card up our sleeve. The entrance door on our side is boarded up so no one can come in. When we arrive at the cafeteria, we find our table.

I notice out the corner of my eye that the leaders are all present and start heading towards us. "Valerie."

It's Rain. I stand up and turn around. "Paige said you missed afternoon-tea. You hungry? Actually… where were all of you?"

I go to speak, but Kelsey cuts me off. "It's not easy dragging our friend through the snow you know?! A fainted body is dead weight! We were exploring the woods we trained in as we wanted to see it for more than just a training zone."

"Oh, she fainted. I see, but why didn't you alert Security?" Rain responds, narrowing her eyes. "Well, you can eat anyway, Valerie. Sorry, my daughter was cruel, but I truly hope tomorrow will be better because we won't be so lenient next time with you for refusing a demand that came from us regardless if it was a cruel 'joke'" she adds on, giving the side of my face a slight clap, then leaves. Dinner is now on and we head to collect a tray each of food.

All our bodies are sores from training and I hope we don't have to go through the same thing again tomorrow, but this time I won't be stupid and actually eat and drink properly. I'll faint for real otherwise so Kelsey's lie will no longer be a lie. It'll be our reality.

Chapter 7

- -

"**S**herbert, why would you do that? It's so unlike you! Sebastian, you should have stopped her!"

I could hear different voices of different genders and tones all around me.I don't know much, but what I do know is that the people these voices belong too are NOT my friends!Blinking open my eyes slowly to see a needle that's been inserted into my left arm connected to a solution of some sort. I try to move that arm, but it doesn't respond. I move my eyes over to see what else is going on. Sebastian, Rain, Harriet, Owen and Shelby are all present.

"W-what? N-no, why..." I choke out which seems to get their attention.I try sit up, but I'm pushed down by Owen and Harriet.

"You're okay now, Valerie." Owen tells me.

"You got tangled pretty hard out there to then be knocked out..."Harriet whispers.

I can feel a semi-uncomfortable pillow slipped under my head to go with a pillow that's already there to help prop me up. Trying to focus my senses, I glance back to Owen and Harriet. A small bright light makes me squint my eyes. Owen pulled a pen light from his pocket. "Can you see okay?" He asks me. I shake my head 'no' and I see him reach to something out of my distance and next thing I know, a light that had actually been on above me has been dimmed.

"That better?"

I nod my head."Good, good."

"So are you going to apologize to her, Sherbert?" I hear Harriet mumble. "W-who-who's Sherbert?" I question. "That... would... be... me. I-I don't know if you've heard Miss Harriet here, calling me that before." I hear Shelby stutter and she has a pet cat on her lap. Since when did she have a pet cat?

I try to sit up again. Owen and Harriet help me out this time, but I push them away indicating I don't want their help."Why'd you do it?" I ask while holding a hand to my forehead that's now pounding.

Shelby rubs her arm and looks away from me. I see Harriet shake her head in clear annoyance.

"So you're going to attack me and not offer an explanation why?!" I snap. The girls turns head to look at me and I see a look of anger in her green eyes. She jumps up and I see her pull out a shovel from a holster on her back and point it in my direction. "I don't OWE you anything!"

I hear Harriet gulp next to me and step back a bit. Owen looks shocked. "Mum, Dad!" He whispers. "Okay sugar-pie, that's enough. Uh... It's time for dinner actually. Let's get you some. Does your cat, Declan want some milk?" Rain questions in a lighter tone, standing up and guiding Sherbert from the room who carries Declan in her arms, away.

I turn and glare at Sebastian. "Oh, don't give me that look, Sprout."

I just cross my arms. "Okay, okay, okay, people. Let's stop... fighting...?" Harriet stammers. I take a good look at her and it dawns on me. "You!" I shout.

"Me?!" She say's looking a taken back.

"Yes!"

"Listen, Valerie, I know what you're thinking and -"

"No! Just shut up! Because of you, me and my friends are trapped here!"

"I'd keep that attitude of yours in check If you can. Because I can tell you now it won't be getting you far with us, or me." I hear Sebastian threaten and he has a bunch of my hair pins, including the one clip I had that stood out.

"Those are mine!" I cry. "Okay, okay, just stop there, Valerie. I can tell you're feeling pretty angry, hurt and betrayed which is understandable, but if you'll allow me to offer some kind of explanation, I can -" Owen begins, trying to intervene.

"Agh! Just get this whatever is in this needle out of my arm and I'm going!" I yell. Even Sebastian looks shocked now. He better be scared of me!

"Okay..." Owen says shortly and he removes the needle from my arm. "It was water I was giving you."

I say nothing. "Eh... I'm hungry too. I'm going to go, uh... follow 'Mum' and Sherbert. Bye!" I hear Harriet announce suddenly before backing away slowly, then running from the room as fast as possible.

"Harriet!" I hear Owen panic. Now, it's just him, Sebastian and me.

"Can I explain?" Owen questions. I just glare. "...I'll take that as a 'yes'"

He grabs a nearby chair and sits down. "That is Shelby, but sometimes we call her Sherbert. She can be uh, rather troubled somedays... I apologize for her attacking you like that..."

"Is she apart of the 'let's screw with our members' for fun?" I hiss. "Uh, yes. Yes, she is. We did have another Guard before, but... well Shelby replaced her so to speak and said 'Guard' was de-emoted."

"'Replaced her'? Who was 'her'?"

"Oh, you've met her, Sport. She's doesn't seem very fond of you, heh. Can't say the same for her teammate and cousin though, Avery. Usually well behaved, but since 'your' arrival, I'm not in a good mood."

I sit there feeling shocked at what I'm hearing. "You know what? This is all too hard for me! I'ma just go..." I trail off sliding my feet to the floor. "Wait!" I hear Owen call and his hand grasps my arm.

"?????"

"You can leave the Hospital, but take it easy... If you can. It was reported earlier by one of the Guards that you passed out in the dining hall, apparently in the woods and to just be knocked out now... Well, and considering the state you and your friends were found in, in the place we call a 'gate-way', I'm glad you all are... okay, to say the least. You haven't had an easy time since arriving here."

"Uh, no! I don't 'faint' regularly, not ever!"

"You sure? I know your type well, Valerie..."

"...." I narrow my eyes a bit and let my mouth drop a little. "Just... take it easy, Valerie, okay?. Sebastian, her and her friends since coming here haven't had a real chance to ease into life here and now were pushing them to compete in a sort of tournament for fun is determinant to each and everyone of their physical health and mental well-being, wouldn't you agree?"

"What?!" I hear Sebastian ask, perplexed. "I say we should give them a few days to get some strength back, rest and put some weight on. They aren't going to be at... their best to go out there and compete."

"Agh, fine."

"Well, there you have it, Valerie. You and your friends, try and get some strength back and rest well, eat, drink. All that stuff."

I nod and take a good look at Owen and he has a warm smile on his face. I can't resist blushing and feeling like my chest is beating a million miles a minute. His so... different to his group, not heartless. Rain is condescending, Sebastian is underhanded, Shelby... She's just hurtful, and Harriet is just two-faced?

"Valerie?" Owen speaks up, clearing his throat. "Sorry, tired." I apologize.

"That's okay. You take care all right?"

"Yes."

"Great. You have a nice night, okay? I... Well I'm hungry and I've got some food waiting for me with my name on it too, heh." Owen laughs, standing up to walk out the door. It's just me and Sebastian now. I gulp and look at him. He has a smirk on his face.

"Sebastian...?" I whisper slowly.

"Valerie." He says back to me, likewise. "You better be careful here, Sport. Because, take it from me. People around here, let alone on other teams to you are not your friends. They are only looking out for themselves, heck1

They are not even looking out for their team-mates. If you think you and your band of friends are going to stay tight close and knitted, you think wrong, heh. You'd be surprised how easily even the best of 'friends' will turn against each-other if it means an advantage, or a way to 'get ahead' so to speak.

Take this advice from me, you'll need it and don't even think of trying to get one up over me or my family, 'us.' We won't stand for it. Come." And he grasps my forearm, pulling me to my feet and leads me down a corridor that were no longer in what looks like a hospital. The further we go, the darker and colder it gets. There's almost no windows now. I see cobwebs are everywhere. I don't like cobwebs, they remind me of the way the orphanage was run before Princess Sophie's Mother's reign ended.

"What is this place?" I ask. Sebastian gives me a look and keeps walking. He has his hands behind his back and just keeps walking. "Do you remember my wifey trying to teach you a lesson?"

"Not exactly..." I whisper, not wanting to speak to loudly. The way he said what he said is... unsettling.

"Stop here." He commands all of a sudden and walks over to a door. We are at the end of the hallway. "Do you know how far down we are, Sprout?"

"Down? As in under-"

"Underground? Yes."

I gulp. I see Sebastian just smirk at my fear. "Are you cold down here?"

"Yes." I respond, trying not to show fear. "That's cute, Valerie. Trying not to show fear, makes you almost as cute as a young woman we used to have here. And by the way, we don't like members wasting food or being ungrateful for what we give them. Now, walk ahead of me. There's something I want you to see."

If he thinks I'm going to show my emotions, he has another thing coming!

"And, I'm not here to help you get ahead. Anything you need done or want help with, learn to do it yourself or ask someone who is a friend. You're an asset, were not. This afternoon was a rarity as I was feeling charitable."

I just keep my mouth closed. "Quiet? Good. You've learnt to keep your mouth shut. If only your 'friends' or the other members here were as smart as you. Now!"

This man might officially be worse than Sophie Ender's mother... Sebastian walks over to a door and lays a hand on it. "Take a look, Sprout, go on."

I walk slowly up to it, to see a small viewing window is built into it. I need to stand on my tippy toes, but I manage to look in and what I see chills me to the core.

"It's Avery!" I gasp, turning to look at Sebastian. I look back up and see her huddled on a camper bed with only a thin blanket and a floppy pillow. She is shivering and I can see her skins blue, but face red from crying. It's somewhat dark in there too...

When Sophie's mother punished people, she never it took this extreme...

"W-why?" I manage to choke out. All this cold air down here has now frozen my voice box and breathing a little. "It's simple. Others are not supposed to help others out there. You're better off looking out for only yourself here, Sprout. Helping others will only bring you deceit and treachery."

All I can do is try not to shake and I try to keep a straight face. "Go on, you can cry."

If he thinks that I'm going to giving him the satisfaction of crying, his got another thing coming!

"You're a resilient one, Valerie despite thinking you're not. I can see it in your eyes. You wish to guard your heart and all the emotions, thoughts, desires and most of all... Your fears you keep locked up inside. Now, you've seen what happens when people don't 'play games', our game in particular, let this serve as your warning not to test me again."

"I understand, I'm very sorry, Sebastian." I tell him.

"Apologetic? Good, good. You'll go far Sprout from now on, oh... but, eesh... I just worry that you may go back on your words. I said you were resilient and I'm not sure our little chat is enough to solidify 'things', so perhaps a demonstration of what we can do will concrete it for sure."

"What are you talking about?" I manage to get out, but it's too late as Sebastian seizes my arm and pulls me to the door next to where Avery is and pushes it open. "Goodnight,

Valerie!" And he shoves me in, locking the door behind me and I hear his cackles fade as he seemingly leaves.

"No!" I shout standing up and running the door, pounding on it, but I don't think it does any good. I turn to the direction Avery should be in and shout her name and earn no response. Soundproof? They'll let me out in the morning, right? Us... out? Samantha tried to warn us about this.

I look over to the camping bed with a floppy pillow and thin blanket of it's own. Guess I have no choice, but to try and sleep through the night. I head over and curl up into a ball, trying to imagine and dream that I'm back home in the orphanage, surrounded my friends and classmates, under the protection of Sophie's democracy.

She, Solayo and everyone is probably worried about me, Louis, Kelsey and Cloud having gone missing and to top it all off, Louis, Kelsey and Cloud don't know where I went after being transported to Hospital. Oh Core, I hope Sebastian isn't going to hurt them!

It's hard not to stop the tears from falling and sliding down the corners of my cheeks. It's been so long now and all the feelings I was keeping bottled up, come flooding out and I cry myself sleep eventually while tracing my finger along the camping bed's metal frame. As I do, something scratched into one of the bricks that makes up the walls of this room has a name, 'Scout Hayes.'

I'm guessing this cell used to be theirs and they were released or they are... I gulp, daring not to even think of the alternative outcome.

Chapter 8

I feel my tears sliding down my face and meeting my knees. It's so cold and I curl up more to try and stay warm. My clothing and my thin blanket doesn't keep me as warm as it should. I look at my hands, seeing the scratches and dried blood all over them from pounding and scratching at the door for hours at one point.

It was a stupid idea for an escape attempt out of sheer desperation.

Then I hear the sound of a door being thrown opened but it's not my own. "Get her out of here."

"No, no, no! What about her?! WHAT ABOUT HER TOO?!"

I hear a series of screams that vanish. They sound like they only get fainter.

"Oh, stop hanging onto the walls!"

That sounds just like Avery! "Valerieeeee!"

I jump up from my 'bed', swinging my legs to the floor, my raven hair cascading down my face to frame it. That was Avery, no!

Then my door swings open and in walks Rain. "Good... Morning, Valerie. How did you sleep?"

It seems like she wants nothing to do with me. How does she want me to even respond this? What does she even expect me to say?!

"Valerie!" I hear her growl, scaring me, making me a jolt a little bit in fright.

"Uh, it, it's cold in here, I couldn't sleep." I stammer.

"That's to be expected. I see you've been crying."

"What? Me, crying? No wayyyyy..." I lie

"I'm not stupid, but, heh, you've suffered." She taunts, pointing to my injured hands.

"Can you just go away, if all your here to do is taunt me?"

"You want me to leave? Fine. I'll just leave you in here then for being rude to me. Doesn't affect my day what so ever!"

And she starts to leave, closing the door behind her. I jump to my feet and pound on the door. "No, no, no, no! Please don't do that! My friends will be worried around me!"

I can feel fresh tears, falling down my face. "Fine, but move away from the door or YOU will get hit in the head by it. I step back to let her open it again. "What are we going to do with you, Valerie?" She huffs with her hands on her hips. I see a loose strand of her pure white hair with a few aqua blue and light green streaks fall into her face and she blows it with her lips, then quickly tucks it behind her ear, flawlessly.

"Rain-" but she doesn't give me a chance to finish, before grabbing my wrist and pulling me out. "That hurts!" I cry.

"That's the point, now shut up!"

I wince at the pain. "You don't have to do this! Why don't you guys just let me and my friends go and we can be on our way. Out of your hair!"

"Nope. Not fun for us if we did that, Valerie."

"Ugh, you're so-"

"So, what?" And I feel her go behind me, taking my both my wrists in hers, pulling them up to hurt me. "Stop!"

"Just keep walking. The sooner I drop you off back at the city center, I can go about starting my day. Your lucky, my Husband has decided to let you and your team off, for a couple days to 'recover' as you've been all slacking the last couple of days. Seems like you're not cut out for fun & games, but I'd like it if you were.

I expect better later. Oh, and no helping others who aren't on your team.

Finally, Rain brings me to the boarding house and she lets go, shoving me to the floor a few apartments down from my apartment. I feel carpet burn. "Your pathetic, Valerie. Can't even stay on your own two feet. I wonder what Solayo ever saw in you for you to gain a place in his class.

Anyway, you won't be going home by any means. Your family *may* have a chance if were feeling generous at any stage, but you? Haha, no. Two left feet. Sorry, no mercy, babe."

And she walks away, leaving me. I see one of the other Guards stepping to block the corridor after Rain has left. I pick myself up. "Why?"

"You don't compete do a job, participate in their games, but aren't disqualified? Your stay here."

"But what are we to do about food???"

"Owen or someone will bring something up for you and your friends. Now shove off!"

I sigh and walk to the end of the corridor where me and my Friends are staying, slowly turning the handle and pushing the door open. I hear the sound of something hitting the floor and I feel two arms wrap around my neck. "Valerie!"

It's Kelsey, she's crying. "Kelsey, I-I-"

She's sobbing, softly into my shoulder and neck. "Where we you?" Louis asks, who's holding a drawing pad in his hands. "I second that, hmph!" I hear Cloud scoff.

I feel myself shaking and seize my arms around Kelsey tighter to deepen the hug. "Oh, Core! Louis! She's crying, we made her cry..." I hear Cloud stammer.

"Valerie, are you okay? Tell us what happened to you." I hear Louis ask.

"Valerie, I-I was so worried about you! You got knocked out by Shelby and were taken by this community's sadistic and psychopathic leaders and didn't return. What happened? They took Avery as well, she gave Security a good fight." Kelsey asks me, stepping back. Hands still on the side of my arms though.

"K-Kelsey, I-I-" I stammer, before feeling dizzy all of a sudden and loosing balance on my feet and nearly crashing to the floor, but she has me though thank goodness before everything goes dark for me.

I feel a pair of cold hands running themselves across my forehead. They are crisp, but gentle.

"How is she?"

"She's goanna wake up, right?!"

I know those voices. It's Louis and Kelsey. I shift my body and can feel a giant pillow behind my head. My guess is they moved me to my bed?

"She'll be fine. She…Just seems like she's been through the ringer is my guess, but bare in mind that I'm no doctor. I'm just a teachers aid and I have only minimal first aid training."

And that's Cloud voice. "Agh! Why can't we ever catch a break?!" I hear Kelsey grumping.

"Why can't I catch a break?" I mumble. "Valerie!" I hear my friends shout. I open my eyes, but the harsh light hurts and I wince. I bring my hand to cover my eyes, but I feel a hand bring it back down the pillow. They are gentle, but kind of strong about it.

"Don't try to move, Valerie." I hear Louis say. "What happened?" Kelsey asks me. I try to sit up a it, but I'm unsuccessful and just slump back down on the bed. I finally open my eyes to see Cloud above me. "Was that you?" I ask. He nods. "We should see if we can get a doctor up here from the Hospital. She doesn't look okay." I hear Louis state.

"Doctor? Doctor?! You think they are going to bring a doctor up here if we ask? No way in hell, Louis!" I hear Kelsey yell.

"Well, it was just a thought." Louis fires back with, both of them beginning to figjt.

"Oh, will you two shut up?!" I hear Cloud snap over the top of them. "We may not have a doctor, but we do have me!"

"True, true. You're right." I hear Louis answer. "Okay, fine." I hear Kelsey say, crossing her arms and I see her sit down on the bed next to mine alongside Louis. He wraps his arms around her. "Why did this sort of thing happen to us? We don't deserve this." I hear Kelsey whimper.

"That's magic for you..." Louis replies, letting out a sigh. "And maybe I don't wanna be magical. Our powers removed might have been a gift. If we get them back ever and go back home, I'll pray to the Core to strip me of them and give me a normal, human life." Kelsey tells him.

"Well, whatever you decide for the long term, Kelsey...We've been selfish." Cloud, butt's in with. "What do you mean?" She questions.

"Oh for god sake! Look at her! Look at, Valerie! She's too unwell to go on!" Cloud snaps.

"What happened to you Valerie last night?" Louis asks me.

"H-he, th-they, ah!" I wince in pain. "Did they hurt you?" Cloud asks me with puppy dog eyes that are actually full of concern for me.

I nod my head. "Not just me." I choke. "Not just you?" Cloud repeats. I nod.

"Avery."

"Oh, god." I hear Kelsey say, bringing her hands to her mouth. "Okay, I think we really need a plan here. We need to be smart with whatever it is we do next." Louis says.

"Just get me out of here! I don't care what we do next!" I cry out, feeling my heavy limbs.

"Okay, we'll do that." Cloud says looking down and rubbing my forehead like a Dad would. "It's goanna be okay, Valerie."

"He's right. We're your friends." I hear Cloud say. "I'm not giving up on you, Valerie. You've always be there when I've needed you actually, helping me out with class and it's about time I repaid the debt somehow!" Kelsey smiles.

"T-thank you." I choke out.

"So, what do we want to do?" Cloud questions.

"My guess is we need to escape obviously..." Louis trails off.

"Hey! We can do that, but go where? If you haven't noticed, Louis we don't have a Core access terminal to get back home and were in the middle of a snowy woods terrain! If we go out there with Valerie in this condition? She won't survive the night!" Kelsey yells.

"And if we stay here, she'll only get worse!" Louis yells back to her.

"Hey, come on now! You both are better than this!" Ivor intervenes. "You guys are the new generation of where we came from still. Now, I know it's not easy, but you guys can't give up! I've seen with my own two eyes what you're capable off!" Cloud smiles, clapping his hands.

I see them exchange glances. "You're right, I'm sorry." They say to each-other. "Finally. Now we're getting somewhere!" Cloud smiles, again.

"We need to get back up to the gateway we were in. There's other star-gates to go through. Maybe one leads back home? We'd have to put all our effort into hoping into each one though." I groan.

"Valerie, I think you should stop straining yourself. You've done enough. Leave this to us." Cloud says gently, rubbing my head again.

"Well, there must be a way back up. The people here, running this place. Harriet was it? She was up there when she pushed us in here, so there must be a way back up." I hear Louis suggest.

"Yeah! You're right! Umm, let's see, let's see. Maybe if we could get our hands on some rope and a hook we could try and throw it up onto the platform we were originally on, perhaps?" I hear Kelsey suggest. It's a long shot, but gates have edges."

"Yeah, good plan! Just how do we get our hands on that stuff without arousing suspicion?" Louis responds.

"Good point, Louis. Ummm... maybe there is a set of stairs or a passage up there from the head of these 'games' side?" Kelsey follows with.

"Let's just leave it to these two, hey?" Cloud whispers in my ear, still rubbing my head. I pull the blanket up around me a bit and I feel him tuck me in. "It's going to be okay."

I nod, feeling tired. "You take a nap. You've earned it."

"Bed-sheets." I mumble. "What?" Cloud questions me.

"If we can't ahold of rope, it's always another possibility." And then I feel myself drift off to sleep.

"Valerie."

"Valerie, wake up."

"Eh?" I let slip, rolling over onto my side to see Cloud. He helped me to sit up and I saw I was still on my bed, where I had been left. "Have a good sleep?"

"I don't want to anyone hurt me!"

"You're okay here, no one's going to hurt you."

"I don't want anyone to hurt me!" I scream, pushing Cloud away from me. I see my action startle Louis and Kelsey who leap up from their beds. They must have been resting. "Woah,

woah, woah! Calm down!" I hear a voice I don't recognize. I turn around to see who.

"Harriet." I growl. She puts her hands up. "Hey, hey, hey. It's okay. You're okay. We can talk can't we?"

Cloud turns away his head, looking visbly uncomfortable. She's so diffrent from what we were told about her by Cloud. Why didn't her soul reincarnate into another identity?

And then I feel something hit me smack bang, Avery. She's a older version of Avery who was the Princesses, Girlfriend's friend!

I've never really stopped to talk to the older generation who were the last to ender the reign of the Princesses Mother, but I've seen photos. Avery was about 25 years old, but in this world she looks as if she's 29 or so.

Why didn't her own soul transition also? I meet Cloud's eyes. He knows, he actually knows! Do Kelsey & Louis not recognize Harriet much or Avery at all?

"Valerie." I heart Harriet snap, raising her voice a little, breaking me out of my thoughts. No matter who Harriet was before, she's no longer a good person now. Not in this world at-least...

"No! You are responsible for us all ending up here and being trapped here! Your worse than every one of your friends!"

I raise my fists to fight her when I feel someone grab my wrists together and put me under their arm pit to stop me. This way, it was impossible to fight. All I could do was struggle.

"Let go!" I shouted seeing Ivor sitting on the floor so it's not him. "Who are you?!" I yell.

"I'll let you go, if you calm down."

"Fine!" And I feel some gently drop me onto my bed, stomach and face first. I take a deep breath and then sit up to see who it was. "Owen?!" I gasp seeing him here. "Good Afternoon, Valerie"

"Afternoon, but I-"

"It's lunch time... Harriet and I brought you and your friends lunch."

I feel anger bubbling inside me and lay back down. "Get out of Our room. I don't want either of you anywhere near me or my friends!"

"Well, I am sorry you feel that way. I do hope with time you will forgive us though."

I say nothing. "Let's just go, Owen. Enjoy lunch, you guys..." I hear Harper say and she leaves with Owen. When they are gone I sit up. "Valerie, what was that?!" I hear Kelsey yell. "Hey! Don't take it out on her!" Louis yells back, going up to Kelsey.

"Dear God, you both are at it again!" I hear Cloud grumble, standing up. He grabs a plate with some sandwiches and a cup of water for me. "You should eat. Get your strength back up, Valerie."

I eat the food, ignoring a pain in my stomach and Cloud eats his. Eventually Louis and Kelsey calm down and eat theirs. After lunch, Louis stacks our plates and cups on one of the dressers in the room. "Um, so, Valerie..." I hear Kelsey whisper.

"Yes?" I respond.

"We have a plan..."

"Okay..."

"We were given sheets to change our beds with and they said with the old ones to pop it down the laundry shoot. We've changed our beds and yours... we tied all the sheets together to make a rope like you suggested. We managed to make some kind of grappling hook out of bending cuterly and some other stiff we found around the boarding house...

Don't ask how..."

I hear Louis snicker and a small smile presents it's self on Kelsey's face. "We will back in the Hallway and can go into the other star-gates. Better than starving in the hallway and I guess sometime risks need to be taken.

What do you think of the plan? We'll be safe there and alive... During that time we can get help to figure out if there is another star-gate for our home. What do you think?" Louis questions.

"It's fine. Just how do we get out of our sleeping quarters?"

"Well, uh... We can go down the laundry shoot? No one will be doing anything wherever that ends up during the night."

"What do you think of Louis's plan, Valerie?" I hear Kelsey question.

"No, Kelsey. It's your plan too." Louis tells her. "It's fine, it's fine. Can I go back to sleep now? I'm tired." I tell them, feeling myself dosing off again.

"Sure, and we'll be right here, Valerie." I hear Cloud tell me before I dose off again.

"Valerie, wake up. It's 1 a.m. You slept throughout the whole day."

I feel someone shaking my knee and I open my eyes to see it's Kelsey. "We need to go, now."

She helps me out of bed. I can feel how much pain my bodies in. "Kelsey, my body hurts alot."

"Want me to carry her?" I hear Cloud ask.

"That will slow you down and her on your back might mean you and her are more easily seen, not to mention vulnerable." Louis steps in with.

"True, but I could carry her bridal style if need be? She's in no condition for escaping really."

"We don't have that sort of time, Cloud right now!" I hear Kelsey respond.

"Come on, Valerie."

Kelsey brings me over to Louis and we swap the clothes I'm wearing for a long shirt, long pants, thick socks, snow boots and a hoodie, plus scarf and beanie. It's embarrassing my friends have to help me dress, but I can barely move my sore limbs. Louis has a bag on his back. I can see the bed sheets hanging out the top a little. I see Cloud pocket the home-made grapple hook. I have no idea how Louis and Kelsey managed that, but if I they think it will work... Then I believe in them!

After this, Kelsey slowly opens the door, looking out. "Coasts clear."

And he goes first. Kelsey is holding my hand in hers. We go together and Cloud. follows. As we are sneaking through the hallway, Louis steps on a creaky floor board.

We all gulp and freeze to see if any Guards come or if any teams wake up. We see we are right in-front of Samantha's team's room.

After a few seconds, we proceed to keep going and make it to the edge of our community and break a hole in the fence. I'm glad it's not electrified.

"It's too quiet, Louis." I hear Kelsey whisper. "I know, I know. I don't like it either." Louis responds. "Shh, both of you." Cloud whispers.

'If we were being watched we would not have made it this far."

"Or they know what we are up too and are up waiting to ambush last minute after we've developed a false sense of security." Louis snaps with quietly. "Let's just keep going!" Kelsey says quietly and she pulls me along. Louis puts his bag on the ground carefully and pulls out the bed sheets tied together. Cloud hands him the grapple. I can see the edges of them have been sharpened which means a great chance of them digging into the ledge up above.

He swings it in a circle ready to throw it up into the star-gate which should send it through to the other side. Kelsey places me in-front of her, but keeps her hands on my shoulders. Cloud to the side of us. All of us ready to start climbing up the bed sheets.

Next minute I hear a small 'dink' and we see a small flash of light come through the sky above and I see Louis has managed to do it. He gives the bed sheets a tug to make sure it's sturdy.

"Valerie, you go first." Kelsey whispers. Louis hands the end to me. "Why, me?" I ask.

"Because if we get caught, at least you will escape." Kelsey answers. I take the rope and start pulling myself up carefully. Kelsey goes next and she helps shove me up it a little, then Louis, followed by Cloud. As were climbing, but before we really get into the portal, I hear a whistle and we all freeze and look down. A torch light appears walking through the area. "Sh-" I hear Cloud say, but stops himself.

A person comes into view. They have a serial killers mask on. Or course! "It's Shelby!" I hear Kelsey gasp while doing it quietly. "She patrolling?" Louis whispers. "Maybe." Cloud grumps from down below all of us. Our hearts beat strongly together, praying she doesn't look up.

After what feels like forever, she leaves the room. We continue climbing and we make it almost to the top tier when I hear a 'riiiiiiipppp' sound. "I don't like the sound of that!" I hear Louis says. "Me, neither..." Kelsey responds. I look up and see the rope is breaking from this much weight on it at one time.

"Can we jump for it? Portals defy logic and gravity." Kelsey questions. "Maybe!" Louis esponds. "Right, Valerie, we need you to jump as far as you can!" They tell me together. I try and I feel my hands grasp the edge of the ledge. "I'm on it!" I whisper down to them. "But I'm slipping!"

I try and pull myself up, but can feel the last of my strength quickly leaving me alongside the rim of the gate being slippery. I hear a sound and I see Kelsey land beside me on the ledge. Next minute it's Louis and finally Cloud. I hear a 'dink' sound and the grapple falls to the ground along with the bed sheets making a muted 'dink' sound. "At least were up." Kelsey says and I see her and Louis climb out of the portal, balancing on the edge of the star-gate's rim.

They each have a hand out. "Valerie." Kelsey says. I take hers and then Louis grabs my other hand. They pull me up and next they help Cloud.

"We've done it!" I say, smiling. "We have." Louis responds. "We make a pretty good team if I do say so myself!" Kelsey speaks with a grin. "See? You three underestimate your-selves!" Cloud whispers.

We start walking and see the stairs we came up. I begin to head towards it when I feel a force tugging on me. "What?!" I scream out loud to see Cloud struggling similar to me. "Valerie!" I hear Louis and Cloud scream. Cloud somehow breaks free and runs over to me, wrapping his arm around me.

Then I see Louis and Kelsey thrown like rag dolls back the way we came. I can see their shock and pained expressions as they fall slowly.

"Valerie, we need to go! Now!" Ivor tells me. "What about them?!" I cry "We can't think of that right now!" And Cloud starts pushing me down the stairs when we hear a loud 'tha-whoomp!' sound a viewing screen appears in front of us.

We see Kelsey and Louis have landed on each-other below, but are live. They look bruised though. "Cloud, they're not moving!"

"Valerie!" He grumbles, trying to get me to continue.

And then I feel a force tug both of us back strongly to the broken rim, threatening to toss us like our friends were so we'll meet the same fate. Cloud and I share a look, deciding controlling our destiny is better than letting someone else control it.

He places a hand on my shoulder, stretches his other arm out and I stretch both of mine, feeling a wind sweep through our hair, tugging at our clothes still and nipping our skin.

Then let ourselves fall back. We make it back rather quickly and hit the ground, but not injured completely. Feels like were floating a bit, saved by someone's powers. I start to black out though, but not before hearing some scary words.

"We heard the rim crack." It's Shelby.

Crap, we've been caught! Is my final thought before I black out. I feel my head hit Cloud's face which is what knocks me out I think. I hope his okay...

Chapter 9

"She's not dead is she?!"

"I don't know if someone could survive that in her condition. She was already not well off. She hit the back of her head on your face, Cloud. You only have minor facial bruising."

I hear voices, but they don't sound like the leaders which is a relief. I slowly open my eyes to see my friends. "This is a relief!" I gasp.

"Valerie!" I hear my friends gasp. Kelsey slips her arm under my back, helping me to sit up slightly. I notice I am on a couch.

"Where are we?"

"Take a look." Louis tells me. I look around to see it's the hidden room we found. "Is the door still locked and barricaded?" I question.

"Yeah, it is. We checked." Kelsey responds. "We were so worried about you, Valerie!" Louis whispers.

"I-I'm sorry, but I'm okay now."

"No, Valerie. It was our fault! More than anything. Don't blame yourself, please!" Kelsey begs me.

"Yeah, our fault. Were so glad your awake now, though!" Louis adds on.

"Valerie, if you had died-I-I don't know what I woulda done-"

"Kelsey, stop, please. It's fine. I'm okay... just, ah... Sore." I tell her. She nods shamefully. Louis does as well.

I look around the observatory. "Where's Cloud?" I ask, noticing his not nearby.

"I'm right here, Valerie."

I look to a sink in the corner of the room to see Cloud. He's holding a tissue to his nose.

"You landed on me, almost broke my nose."

"I'm sorry!" I cry. Cloud takes a seat near us. "Don't worry, it's not your fault. It will heal. I've faced worse."

"Worse?" Cloud pipes up with, an eyebrow raised.

"Once you have shared a tent with- Uh, you know what? Nevermind..."

"I don't get it..." Kelsey starts off with, but Cloud cuts her off with. "Anyway, Kelsey! We need a new plan because this one didn't work!"

"Can I ask a question?" I interrupt with. They all look at me. "If we tried to escape... Don't we need to get to our Room? They'll search this community and we aren't there. Were here..."

"Oh, you're right!" Louis gasps.

Kelsey helps me to stand. "Can you walk?!"

"I-I think."

We all head to exit when we hear a whirring sound. "What is that?" Cloud questions, tapping his fingers against his beard. He goes to the giant telescope and looks through it.

"Very perculier."

"Perculier?" Louis questions with her arms out.

"It's a plane, flying right towards us. Into the airspace of this whole place..."

"What would a plane be doing here?" Kelsey asks. "I don't know..." Cloud mumbles back.

Were all looking out the window now, Cloud still with eye looking through the telescope. We see lights in windows slowly light up outside. The lights that line the cafeteria, hospital, etc light up too.

"Seems that plane woke everyone up." Louis murmurs. questions. "This could be our distraction we need!" I cry out.

"Yeah, you're right, Valerie!" Kelsey whispers to me. "If they are distracted, they won't be looking for us!"

Just then we see some guards down below, outside on the ground looking up to the sky.

One of them looks different though, smaller. "Is that Shelby?" I question, struggling to see as it is dark out.

"It is." Clouds responds quickly. "Wait..."

"What?" I hear Kelsey snap, getting a bit impatient. We all start to back away fron the window, but it's too late and we see her turn around to look up at us. Our eyes meet.

We all gulp. "We need to get out of here!" I gasp.

We take off running through the passengers in the walls and make a frantic dash down a desolate side street as best we can before Shelby comes up here. Kelsey and Louis are helping me to run.

We sneak into the dormitory and I place my hand on the door handle to open the door of our room when I hear a voice.

"Now, look what the cat dragged in."

We all gulp. Kelsey and Louis let go of me to get ready to fight, raising their fists. Solayo taught us magic, but he also taught as other practical skills and even brought guests in sometimes. We learned martial arts from the police chief, Ryland back home. Cloud wraps his hands around me instead in protection.

"Woah, friends, relax! Were all chill here!"

I turn around looking to see who. It's Avery & Samantha. "Avery!" I squeal, throwing my arms around her neck. She returns the hug.

"We thought you were Shelby!" Cloud says, stepping forward.

Samantha rolls her eyes. "I don't like that girl."

"Does anyone?" Kelsey says sarcastically. I see Samantha smile a bit and Kelsey returns it.

"Ah, Valerie, I was so worried about you!"

"Avery, I was too! What happened to you was my fault!"

"No one was at fault, alright?!" Grumps Samantha.

"Can someone explain what's going on? And the extent of what happened to Valerie and Avery?" Louis begs.

"Sebastian just got angry, he does alot. When he needs to blow off steam, he picks a victim to incur his wrath." Avery answers.

"But Valerie was freezing cold and sleep-deprived and starving!" Kelsey yells. "Being taken underground is a scary place, but thank god it wasn't worse, worse if you know what I mean." Avery responds, trying to he dismissive.

"Worse?" Louis repeats.

"I don't want to talk about it..." Avery trails off with. She let's go of hugging me.

"You all should get changed into your PJ's asap so it looks like you were sleeping." Em says.

"Shelby saw us! Changing our pj's might not absolve us." Cloud exclaims. "Yeah..." Cloud answers.

"Just get changed, now! The leaders need to think you were in bed, asleep! It's almost time for curfew to end." Samantha says with a real look of panic on her face. She pushes all into her room.

We hurry to get changed into our pj's

and hang up or tuck away the clothes we were wearing. Good thing we didn't get them muddy. They do have some dust on them though and I see Louis boost Kelsey up and she hides our backpacks in the roof, a tile easily able to be moved aside.

I must have been asleep when they discovered this.

I hear Samantha's voice outside. "Oh, Shelby! Hello, hi, what do us - your loyal members owe your visit?"

I peak out the door while my friends are busy. Avery is nearby and slips inside, pushing me back in. Samantha has her distracted up the other end of the hallway, but Shelby is quickly chewing her out on why her & her team aren't in bed right now.

"Valerie!" Avery whispers. "You all need to get into bed now!"

Cloud, Louis and Kelsey dive into theirs. I jump into mine, but we all notice we forgot the light. Avery runs over, switching it off than dives under my covers to hide.

She's down low near my legs. I can feel her shaking and she has her arms around them, her skin ice cold.

We hear intense knocking.

"Surprise inspection!" We hear Shelby yell as the door bursts open. She walks into the room, a key in her hand.

Kelsey and Louis fake, waking up groggy. Cloud stays pretending to be asleep. So do I.

"Have you all been asleep in your rooms the last few hours?"

"Why are you here in our room? What is it? Like 5 a.m?" Kelsey says feigning a yawn.

"Answer my question, Kelsey!" Shelby snaps, clearly not in the mood for messing around. I see Shelby grab Kelsey's arm, pulling her out of bed and throwing her to the floor. I see her hit her head on the nightstand beside her bed on her the way down through my slightly peeking eyes.

"Kelsey!" Screams Louis. I and Cloud jump 'awake' as there is no way we can ignore this any longer.

"Valerie, Cloud." We hear Shelby say. "What are you doing?!" Cloud yells walking her to her, but she pulls out a metal shovel from a strap on her back, th end pointed from being recently sharpened.

"I wouldn't come any closer if I were you, Cloud."

He freezes. "Good decision." Shelby says sarcastically and then we hear another knock. It's Harriet.

"Sherbert, my 'sister', there you are! 'Mum' and 'Dad' are looking for you! What are you doing here?!"

"Making sure everyone is where they needed to be, 'Sis.'"

"Okay, okay..."

"Agh!" Shelby yells stomping out. Harper looks at us all. "I'm sorry for her barging in here at this hour, guys... Breakfast will be in two hours from now. Go back to sleep if you can."

And Harriet leaves the room, closing the door. We let 10 minutes pass, afraid to move incase this is a trick. Nothing happens and we all hop out of bed. Louia locks the door and I pull the covers off my bed. Avery sits up. "That was a close one! She scares me!"

"She scares me too." I tell her. Avery looks at me. "I need to go back to my room, Valerie. I'll see you at the cafeteria later. Sam is goanna wanna debrief with me."

I watch her leave. A part of me can't help, but feel sad at her departure.

I'm sitting at my groups designated table. Kelsey and Louis look dead tired. It's a good thing the main injuries we have are not visible from underneath our winter gear, but we will have to lie as Cloud's face is bruised and my head's aching.

I feel dizzy a bit. The next thing I know is a hand on my shoulder which makes me jump. I accidentally kick Louis and Kelsey in the shins beneath the table

They both give me a look. "?!?!?!?!?!"

"Now, they are a bit more awake. We lost a few hours of sleep."

"Valerie." I hear a voice. I turn my head to see Samantha. She places a clear cup of water in-front of me.

"Mind if *MY* groups joins yours?"

I go to speak, but just end up resorting to nodding. Samantha, Avery and the other two guys on the team joins us.

Samantha passes other cups of water towards my friends.

"Sooo, how is the morning treating, ya?" Samantha asks with a cruel smirk.

We all nod weakly. "So, I was thinking. How about we all 'team up' to try and win these games even though Sebastian hates team-work between other groups. We can help eachother out you know and be buddies."

"What do you want in return? I feel this isn't just you wanting to piss him off." Kelsey and Louis say together, weakly.

"Oh, nothing, nothing. I just want us to be friends, that's all."

Samantha lowers her head a bit. "I can keep your secret about last night. I know what you guys did. So how about it?"

"You're black mailing us?" Louis says quietly.

"Yep, streaky. So how about it?"

"Fine." Grumbles Kelsey. "Fantastic!" Em smiles and I feel her slap my back. It hurts.

"Attention, attention everyone!" I hear Owen call, appearing. We and everyone else turn our heads. In front of where we get food from is Sebastian, Rain, Sherbert, Harriet & Owen. I see Harriet smile at Shelby, but Shelby just brushes her off with a scowl.

I look to Samantha. She has a small smile on her face. I look over to where she is looking to see Ricky. His smiling too. He stops though when he sees me. Samantha stops and I feel a pressure on my foot for a few seconds, then it stops.

"Ouch."

"Shut it." Samantha says under hear breath.

"I bet you all heard that noise last night, huh? Like a plane engine?" Samantha begins, stepping forward, arms behind his back.

Everyone nods and we do too. "Well, the problem has been dealt with, so don't worry about it. There is no risk to any of you. We'll protect you."

That doesn't feel reassuring. "I want you all to go about your business. Just... last night outside the entrance gate, it seems we had some individuals escape, based on the number of foot-prints in the snow, not to mention the fence was found, cut.

I don't know who of you did it, but this is your home now, all of you so it will serve you well to remember this. Were supposed to be a community.

And don't anyone ever think about escaping ever. You know what lies outside the gates of this community actually? A frozen wasteland. Out there is guaranteed death.

Do you all know what is Merge is?"

Outside isn't dangerous... Well, as far as we've seen. We hear everyone else gulp & some scared whispers are exchanged.

I see Louis mouth to Cloud. "What's Merge?"

Cloud shrugs his shoulders. I don't think he knows. "Think about how good you all have it here. In here you are protected by walls, our guards, have beds of your own and access to food, water, first aid, not to mention, emergency medical attention and even friends.*

I sware Sebastian is smiling at me when he says 'close friends'.

"Most of all, some of you guys get to play games all day! It's much better than working long hours, huh?"

I see Harriet flinch when he says 'work.' Is there something there? I don't know...

"Well, I'll be off. You all enjoy your day and get ready for training today. Valerie's team, you're back into the competition now. What a lovely day today will be, oh, and there will be no breakfast this morning. If one of you misbehaves, you ALL suffer the consequences! Think about the people around you next time any one of you think about escaping!"

After that all the leaders have left. I sware Sebastian and Shelby are staring me down, but without proof... They can't pin it on us.

A minute later, I hear Samantha mumble and Avery sigh. "Not again..." Samantha whispers.

"What do you me-" I start to say, but Samantha shushes me, pressing her fingers against my lips.

"We'll talk later, Valerie."

Samantha and Avery plus the rest of their group rise and go sit back to their table. I look back at Ricky. He has a glass of water in his hands. I see him walk over and hand it to Samantha. They both seem to have a small two second moment and then he leaves, with an annoyed expression again.

"Are we able to have, water?" Louis calls out. "No, none of you! The leaders don't care what orders we, Security impose unless it affects them." Slab grumbles as he walks past us. "And the mere cups Samantha gave you, were letting slide."

I hear Louis sigh and Kelsey throws her head on the table, distraught.

"No... Please not her. Not again..." Kelsey cries.

'Kelsey..." I whisper.

"I'm sorry, Valerie, I'm so sorry!" She cries into her hands, tears flowing.

Chapter 10

Yeah, surrendering is a bad idea. They can't starve us all forever, right? People will die otherwise and then they have no one to rule over. It would be counter-productive for them.

Just as I'm thinking, I hear a knock on our door. Louis and Kelsey groan, rolling off their beds to answer it. "What?" Grumbles Kelsey, opening it to see Harriet.

"Sebastian wants to address everyone. That includes you all too." And then she leaves. I try to stand, but topple straight over. Cloud comes to my rescue and places my arm around his neck to help me walk. I lean on him for support.

When we file out into the hallway, all the members of this boarding house are here in their PJ's. They all looked hungry and tired like us. Training wasn't easy today. As Sebastian addresses everyone, I feel myself shaking.

"You okay?" Cloud whispers to me. I shake my head. "Your blood pressure could be low?" He whispers afterwards. I see Louis and Kelsey exchange a glance.

Are they going to tell?

Louis slowly goes to raise his hand, but Samantha's hand shoots straight up, saving him.

"It was me."

"What?!" Sebastian yells. "I was the one trying to escape." She says again. "And your team?" Rain questions from the side of the hall.

"They have nothing to do with this. Only I was trying to escape." Samantha responds.

"Geez, you'll never change. This is why I'm not friends with you in particular." Shelby speaks up, hissing.

"Alright, let's say I believe you, sprout-" Sebastian begins when I hear a dead weight sound and see Kelsey and Louis lying on the floor on each-other, exhausted.

"Sebastian! This has gone far enough." I hear Owen say, stepping in. I'm glad they aren't all heartless! "Valerie..."

"Cloud?" I answer, weakly hearing him call my name. Next thing I know, we have both hit the floor too from exhaustion. I hear an "Ugh." And I see Shelby roll her eyes. She's leaning against the wall and props her leg. "Sebastian!" Yells Owen again, standing to confront him. I see Harriet smile a bit, walking over to Kelsey and Louis. She helps them up and then moves onto Cloud and me.

"I will handle this problem and discipline with Samantha accordingly." Owen tells him with his arms crossed.

"Fine." Sebastian grumps, walking off followed by Rain and Shelby I see Shelby and Harriet share an angry glare at each-other, but then Harper turns to us with her common warm smile.

"Okay, all of you. Go back to your rooms and rest up. I and Harriet will bring up some food and water up." Owen announces. Everyone nods, walking back to their rooms. Samantha, Avery and their team help me and my friends up quickly, but then leave us. I see Owen along with the Guards and Harriet give us a look.

I think they know it was us. "Valerie... C'mon." Cloud whispers to me, starting to pull me along back to our Rooms.

After another night's sleep alongside some food and water, were feeling better.

I'm sitting at our table in the dining hall. It's really cold out, more than usual. I take a glance around to see how tired, exhausted and cold the other members are. The food and water was something last night, but it's not enough to really help us all feel better completely though.

Then I hear a series of footsteps and clapping. "Good morning my property."

It's Sebastian, Rain and Shelby. All the other competitors stand up except my team. Were beyond caring at this point. Death would be salvation.

"Uh, hello? Get up!" Rain shrieks at us. I see Louis roll his eyes and some of the Guards come walking over to us when I feel someone pull back the back of my clothes to make me stand. It's Samantha.

She gives a quick nod to Ricky who's the leader and they all retreat. "Just behave!" She whispers into my ear in a slightly threatening manner, before going back to her table. I and my friends are now standing.

"Good, now that you are all are standing, Owen and Harriet have taken a sick day today, so it's just us on duty.

Allow me to remind you that these are OUR games and OUR community. We control them and we own YOU. Got it, Sprouts Yes? Good!"

So after last night's fiasco and the fact I don't believe certain so and so's are telling me the truth!"

Sebastian says the last part under his breath. I know it's directed at Samantha "So there won't be food today again till the real escapees come forward. For every day that you's don't come forward, you and your fellow community members will suffer.

Let it sink in a bit, heh."

"No!" I hear Kelsey yell, slamming her firsts on the table and standing up. "Kelsey!" Louis whinges, trying to pull her to sit, but she doesn't budge.

"Anything you want to tell us?" Rain taunts and Kelsey bites her lip.

Sebastian looks angry. "Ricky, remove this immature teenager." He says, signalling to Ricky who grins, approaching her. "Oh, so now you admit that I was formally a teenager?!"

But it does no good.

"Stop!" I hear Avery yell, standing up too. Ricky looks at her, signalling Paige to help out. She starts approaching Avery.

"Fine, anyone who wants to get locked up in isolation too, be my guest. We have more than enough Guards." Sebastian says dismissively, not looking at us.

But not all in the one area... Some are out hunting & scavenging so in this immediate area, there's only 5 of them and like 32 of us. They can't take us all! I wave my hand a bit and I see Louis alongside Cloud stand up.

"Alright, no problem! I pride myself on being resilient then." Sebastian says, still not caring. I look to Samantha and she sighs, standing up too. I see her wave her hands a bit and other member stand up too which scares Sebastian a bit. She has some influence... He looks shocked. I stand up too, lastly.

"You can't take us all." I announce. Sebastian and Rain look beyond fuming now. I see Shelhy shake her head like, 'No, you're stupid' towards, Avery.

Avery looks scared a little. Is there something there too? I feel like everyone in this room has secrets with someone and every here or there, etc.

"Sebastian, this isn't working!" I hear Rain growl at them losing control over us. "I know, I know." Sebastian grumbles back.

"Okay, you know what? You all can go out in the snow and harvest Merge!" Shouts Hadrian and a few Guards trucks drive up.

Who called them?!

Before I know it, we've all been marched out into the snoey woods outside the community. The guards along with half the leaders today are standing around, watching us.

Were all standing in a straight line, wearing plastic medical gloves, hair net and wearing full protective clothing and holding a sack. "Allow me to remind you all and for the ones who are new, if you think about escaping into the winter-land behind you... It's not worth it.

It's just a frozen wasteland out there. There's no civilization beyond here. Got it? And as always I say, safety first.

Merge when it's not been converted, is still growing wild, has dangerous properties. You don't want to end up like how Natasha did, do you?

Good, now all of you start collecting."

I turn around walking with my friends and Samantha alongside Avery and their team. They look upset.

"Sooo, what's the plan?" Louis asks.

"There is no plan. We just have to do this." Samantha responds flatly. "But-" Louis starts off, but she shoots him down. "May I remind you - you're team got US into this!

And we had other members of our group before... One of them was Natasha, Avery's older sister, she died collecting Merge so don't inhale it."

After that we sort of disperse to pulling this long hard white stick that has a crystalized appearance out of the ground.

It has a really strong chemical smell. Good thing we were given breathing masks. "Valerie, with me."

I look up, seeing Samantha waiting for me. "Really?" I ask. "Yes. Now, come on!"

She walks over, grabbing my arm and dragging me. "Sam..."

"What?!" She snaps.

"Can we talk?"

"You can try."

I sigh as we come to a small patch of Merge. "It's really cold out." I tell her. "Yeah, it is..." She responds back, starting to pull Merge out of the ground.

"Can you tell me about this Merge-" But I don't get to finish. Merge is a kind of plant and yes, I know it doesn't look like one. Touching it and breathing it in is only dangerous in it's primary form.

When Sebastian converts it into medicine, it's no longer lethal the smell and to touch, but it still carries some dangerous properties, but you don't need to worry about those unless you consume more than 80ml of Merge once it's converted."

Oh, and word of advice, try not to rip your gloves. Because if the pointed pieces pierce your skin, you'll get an infection and really sick, suffer a fever. You'll start to suffer from hallucinations. It's really quite awful! Sebastian would make an antidote, but you'd suffer in the mean time."

"Okay."

"I can see you have alot of other questions."

"Do the others use it?"

"Uh, no."

"So how much of this do we need to collect?"

"Whenever Sebastian tells us to stop."

"Okay..." I respond quietly. From then on, we just rip it out of the ground for hours on hours. This is worse than training!

I notice around me as time goes on some of the members have given up and are just lying there in the snow exhausted. Sebastian is smirking. It's really only my family and Samantha's friends left.

"How are they going?"

I hear Shelby's voice. "Good, good. I think they will have learnt their lesson soon." I hear Sebastian respond.

"This should teach them about ever standing up to us in the future. Better to suppress the rebellion now before it becomes a bigger problem." I hear Rain answer with.

I feel so angry with them and just clench my fists, but don't get far as I feel a gloved hand touch mine. "Take a few deep breaths, Valerie..."

It's Samantha. She looks tired, but is being gentle. I take a few and watch the cold air when it leaves my mouth through the mask. "Do you feel better now?" She whispers. I nod.

"Good, just remember you can fall back on that when you need it..."

I look off into the distance at the snowy covered mountains. "Don't, his right when he says it's a snow covered wasteland. I think this world just goes on forever. The only life here is us.

Going out there would be suicide."

"You're wrong." I tell her.

"Am I? What proof do you have to support this theory?"

"The plane. It came from some place else... And we come from some place also."

Em looks away from me. "What aren't you telling me? You can trust me, Samantha."

"...My story really isn't worth telling, Valerie."

"Sam."

"What?" She snaps, again.

"Do you know how me and my friends entered this world?"

"I heard rumors, but rumors can just be that. Rumors."

"Stairs. We were wondering a a gateway hall of other star gates and ended up here. It's invisble to the naked eye typically unless you know what you're looking for."

She turns her face with a shocked expression. Seems like I got through to her.

"We could go out searching, Valerie, but the most we might find is a makeshift camp of member who have escaped the community and living out there."

She says, pointing. "Anyway, I don't want to go out there."

"Sam..." I push her and then she looks like she's reconsidering or something.

"I have an idea, Valerie, come here." She says, eyeing Sebastian who's distracted.

"What?" I ask, approaching her when I feel her grab me both my arms. "Sam! What are you doing?!" I panic, trying to flail around.

"Just play along!" She grunts under her breath. She picks me up off the ground it almost hurts. I see we've gotten everyone's attention including the leaders.

"I am going to win Sebastian challenge, you hear me?! I'm strong and you're weak!" She starts shouting at me. "I'll make sure of it that I'm their favorite here on, out!"

"Stop, please! You don't have to do this!" I cry.

"Oh, but you're in MY way and you won't ever stand down!" She yells back.

"Samantha, put my friend down now!" I hear Kelsey yell, raising her fists and Cloud and Louis join her.

"Stay out of this you pipsqueak! You're a weakling! This is between me and Valerie!" Samantha yells back.

"Weakling? Pipsqueak?!" Kelsey yells getting angrier she looks ready to rush at Sam when I see Shelby restrain Kelsey.

"Don't do anything stupid that you will regret later!" She scolds Kelsey "Let go of me!" Yells Kelsey, trying to get out of Becky's grasp.

"No, this is for your own good." Shelby responds. I see Louis grab Shelby's mask that's hanging off her shoulder head and throw it into the nearby lake. Shelby lets go out of Petra and glares at Lukas. She says nothing for a bit then speaks.

"Good thing I have spares. I won't be getting that one back, thanks to you!"

"Why?" Asks Louis playing dumb. "You idiot!" Screams Shelby. "Merge has contaminated this worlds natural water supplies. If I go in there, I'll get sick and maybe even die!"

"The perfect plan!" Sam grins, evily bringing me closer to a lake.

"Stop!" I hear Sebastian yell. "Ricky, Paige, the rest of you! Stop her!"

They grab Sam and I drop to the ground, seeing Rain wrap her arms around me and drag me back, through the snow.b onto me and pull me out from the middle of the snow.

"Enough! Will you all stop fighting?! This is more chaos than usual!" Sebastian yells.

"And I'll do so much worse, destructively if you don't feed any of us." Sam responds back.

"Fine! We'll play it your way, Sprout! I just don't want you actually getting my family and friends or any members killed. That includes injured too.

Take her to isolation! Food is reinstated for the time being, but you ALL will be confined to your quarters from now on!

You hear me?!"

All the member nod. "Good." Sebastian responds. I see Avery approach Shelby. She goes to pat her back when she turns around, grabbing her hand, glaring.

"Sherbet-" Avery starts, but is quickly cut off. "Forget the mask, Avery. It doesn't matter." Shelby tells her.

"But-"

"And were not friends! We haven't been for ages! I don't need friends!" Shelby yells, storming off. Rain and Sebastian look shocked. Ricky's patting Sam's back as they drag her away. Poor Avery bends down crying a little after being left alone.

"Shelby and Avery were once friends? Huh. I wonder what the deal is still with Sam and Ricky?

"Sam used to be one of our guards."

"What?" I say , turning my head forgetting that Rain saved me kind of. "They still have certain affections for each-other. It's nothing big and I personally don't mind a bit of romance in my day."

I look at Rain shocked. "What? And Stop staring! She be-trayed us, so we demoted her to being a farm worker. Don't worry about it. She's hot head like my Hubby and I am too sometimes, but she'll calm down soon. Sebastian as well."

I gulp upon hearing this and close my eyes tightly. "Hey, you okay?" I hear Rain ask, placing her hands on my shoulders. I open them slowly, seeing her pale skin has turned golden slightly and it's like warmth is radiating off of her. And her long blonde hair in a ponytail looks white.

Her eyes look cherry colors rather than blue and doey eyed.

She has a concerned, puzzled expression on her face. "Valerie?" I hear her call my name. I squint my eyes again.

"Do you have a headache? Fever? Not feel well in any way? Maybe you feel like you're going to be sick?

I don't answer her. I feel her pull me into a hug which is odd, lifting me up into her arms. "Sebastian, let's assess Valerie for Merge exposure."

He doesn't protest, nothing and follows her.

Was this all a part of Sam's plan? I don't know, I'm so confused.

Chapter 11

I can hear hushed tones. When I manage to keep my eyes open, I see I'm in a bed in hospital. I'm about to sit up when I feel a hand force me to lay me back down. It's icy cold which can only be one person, Rain.

She used heat magic, but it seems icy is her powers default. No doubt she might be exhausted from doing the opposite, producing warmth.

"Sit down, Sprout or you will make your fever worse."

"Huh?" I ask, trying to sit up.

"Just stay in bed."

And I'm pushed down again, but this time it's not Rain. Sebastian instead. They're both towering over me, dressed like doctors. "W-what happened?"

"You haven't got Merge exposure. Your blood tests came back negative." Sebastian says, somewhat calmly. "Honestly, I AM relieved!" Rain says, placing a damp rag on my forehead.

"Why are you doing this?" I ask.

"Doing what?" Rain answers shortly, but with a confused expression.

"Being... nice?"

"Do you want help or not, pathetic, sorry excuse for an angel?" Sebastian grumbles and I nod my head furiously. "Fine, you're underweight and dehydrated as you obviously know, but you're friends oblivious to it. That's all, but you're also slight cold." He says afterwards."

We just all stay quiet for a bit and then be speaks again, sitting down, throwing plastic gloves his wearing into a bin. "You know, Valerie...

I was actually quite worried about you to tell the truth... For a second anyway. Nothing more, nothing less. Samantha usually carries a quick temper, but I have never seen her behave so irrationally before, especially to pick you up like that and threaten to throw you into the river. It genuinely scared me and my wife."

I nod, not knowing what to say around them because they can be quiet impulsive too. "Well." He says, standing up. "You're fine to go back to your dormitory. I'm retiring for the night." And Sebastian walks out the door without a second though, leaving Rain with me. There is something different about her...

She has her hands clutched together, but they're shaking, her body is hunched over, head hanging low and she's very pale, verging on being blue her skin and her hair has a glassy effect.

Her eyes look dead too. "Rain?" I whisper. She doesn't answer me.

Has she been crying? She starts looking around the room, trying to avoid my gaze. "Rain...?" I ask slowly.

"Yes, Kiki? I-uh, Damn it!" She says grumpily after starting off gently. She almost seemed kind for a moment despite sad and I hear her sigh.

"Come with me, let's get you something to eat and I'll explain. Don't think you're getting special treatment or anything from now on though, Valerie." She huffs to disguise whatever it is, she's going through, and leads me out of the hospital.

She led me to her house that she shares with Sebastian, Owen, Harriet & Shelby.

Walking in behind her, I feel my mouth drop open when I see dark wood floors, chandelier lights, marble benches covered in all kinds of appliances. "Woah! This is really high class, fab and swanky!"

"Well, I'm glad you think so. Always like to hear that we have good tastes in home decor and that our furnishing skills are on point." She chuckles, smiling, her voice small and soft, eyes soft and small too.

She looks at me and gestures for me to follow her. We stop at the fridge and pulls it open.

"We have soft drink, breakfast juice, cordial, cold water, full cream and lactose free milk. Harriet is sensitive to dairy.

And coffee, tea or milo is on the bench." She says, then stands up with her hands on her hips, looking at me with a smile and flicks her ponytail over her back a little with the slight movement of her head ."What would you like?"

"Water."

"What? Just water?" She asks, looking seemingly worried. "Yes." I tell her. "Oh, I see... I forgot you were exactly like, Dana..." She responds, handing me a flask of cold water. She then walks over to a bench, grabbing a bowl. "Soup?"

"Yeah... Just not high calorie..."

"We should talk about this... But okay, there is a lighte calorie soup I can give you." She says, taking a can of soup out of a cupboard, then warms it up for me.

When it's ready, we take a seat together at the island. She has a cup of tea in her hands.

I sit there, unsure what to do. I don't want her to watch me while eating.

"You can eat it, it's not going to hurt you"

I look up to see her looking at me.

"I know." I whisper, "But my heads telling me-"

She cuts me off. "You don't have to explain it to me. Were familiar with anorexia, Valerie."

I cringe when she says this. "For now, why don't we talk and maybe you can try a bite or two in the process? I'd rather you have two bites than not eat anything at all on me.

Is their anything you want to know? I'm not an evil bitch 100% of the time like you think. I can see in your eyes that your soul holds questions."

I hear her sigh. "You called me, Kiki before..."

"Oh, I did..."

"Who's that?"

"Uh, I'm a Mother, Valerie. Let's just say none of my children talk to me or my Husband... And the ones that do, aren't actually ours, biologically anyway. Family is what you make it." She shrugs, trying to avoid the question.

"Who's Dana and Scout?"

"Oh, uh, well, they were once a part of this community, but they're not anymore."

"What do you mean?"

"They're both dead, Valerie. Maybe next time around, they both won't have to die again."

"Tell me more?"

"No."

"Why are you forcing souls to re-live a life they've already lived, but altered?"

"I can't tell you. Why don't you ask normal questions that is in the realm of possibility for me to explain to you, please."

"Okay... Sam and Avery."

"Samantha and Avery."

"Yes."

"Well, Samantha used to be one of our 'Guards', but she stopped taking orders so she was demoted and the rest is history, which is why you don't mess with us, Valerie. Let that be a lesson to you, dear."

"And Avery?"

"Her sister, Natasha died from Merge exposure. She took off her mask and breathed it in. There was no saving her. She died from her lungs being literally burnt from the insides, painful way to go.

And Avery's another pain in the butt like you as far as I am concerned."

"That's not what I meant..."

"Then what did you mean?"

"It seemed like Avery & Shelby were once friends."

"Friends? Ugh, not now, I'll explain. It's an old story though from when we were all younger. Harriet and Shelby used to be good friends, but something happened, we all got dragged into and one of the downsides was, they're no longer friends with each-other now. They hardly ever talk.

Because of that, Shelby searched for friends elsewhere and had a short "thing" with Avery. Now I'm not saying me or Sebastian would discourage it... but... you know what? Nevermind, it's not really any of your business!"

"Why are you being so nice to me?"

"Like I said, I'm not a bitch all the time. No one's born purely evil."

"...."

"I'd disagree..."

"Right... Well, moving on, this is the only reprieve you get, missy! You've had alot and you're being a burden on us. Start pulling your weight, will you?!

Well, her kindness didn't last long... I think I've pushed her as far as she can go.

"I will." I answer quietly and force myself to take bite of the soup, trying to avoid her gaze. I've already have several, not realizing during talking. "Valerie." She says, returning to caring slides a strand of my raven hair out of my face. I see the look of shock in her face though when she's realized what she's done and stands up, with her white, but blue & aqua toned hair hair falling in-front of her face that I can't see her eyes.

"Get out."

"But-"

"Get out, Valerie!"

I panic and stand up quickly. "Just leave." She growls at me and I step out of the kitchen, leaving to head back to my friends. I'm a little confused trying to find my way out when I hear several voices and I hide behind a wall, peering into a room. It's Shelby sitting alone at a dining table.

Declan is on the floor next to them all, sleeping. "Hehe that was such a funny joke, Dan! We should all totally go see it one day, together!" I hear her exclaim happily, kicking her legs in delight, then she reaches out weirdly.

"Aw, thanks for the hug, Libby." She smiles, then begins talking to others, but no one's there.

Is this the true Shelby I'm seeing right now? Suffers from psychosis? Or, just has imaginary friends despite being like in her twenties.

All of a sudden I hear her shriek and she leaps off the table.

"Shelby." I hear an unfamiliar voice say. I panic seeing a male wearing long white pants, has a pink & blue checkered shirt beneath a yellow cardigan and a cat tail and ears are portaging. Shelby looks around for where to go, but he has her cornered.

"W-who are you? Where are my friends friends?! W-where did they go?! Where's my pet cat? Declan! Declan!";

" I hear her say. The man steps forward. "None of it was real, but at the same time it was. You wanted to see what you wanted to see because you were lonely.

You've felt like most people in your life have betrayed you in some way, right? Do you know who I am?" Says the man.

"Declan...?" She suggests, relaxing her body posture.

"Correct, it's me."

"How are you a human?!"

"I'm not a cat, Shelby. I can shift shape. It's a long story, but I had a friend, James He... did something. He was obsessed with you and... Well, it's a long story. He turned me into a vat just as I awakened to what he was doing. You don't need to know though. It's okay because I'm here for you and you don't have to afraid anymore.

To make a very long story short, I'm an Angel from the Core and I'm not the only one. Were working on restoring the many world's in parallel existence to each-other. You don't need to be afraid or alone anymore. No one has to be."

He bends down, reaching out His hand to Her. "Come with me. I can bring you into the Law of Cycles, I won't leave you. Were friends and we have been for a very long time. You've shared your fears with me, your most inner thoughts, your hopes, goals and dreams. I may have been a cat for so long and that this will take getting some used to, but -"

He doesn't get to finish as she throws herself at him, hugging him around the neck. I see tears falling down her cheeks. "D-Declan!"

He just smiles, resting a hand on her head and wraps his other hand around her. "It's going to be okay, I'm here. I've been looking for you for a very long time."

I see a cream colored light that smells of frangapani's and just as they vanish he looks at me, mouthing: "Good luck, Valerie. Help will be along soon to help you."

I can see a circle in my mind with a whole bunch of fate lines connecting the center. I was just privvy to something special...

And then I see a ripple in the middle of the room and I see a ghostly version of Shelby walking away, carrying Declan as a cat in her arms... And then it hits me.

There is a thousand outcomes for just one situation and I witnessed where one two divide. I'm learning more that I did in class, experiencing how the worlds the Core built us, work. Wait... Kiki. Our God is Kiki! I look back to the direction of the kitchen.

No, it's not possible! I tell myself, starting to panic from simply watching outcomes separate themselves from other outcomes and I start running out the door into the snow, back to the boarding house.

Chapter 12

Then I hear a dinking sound and see a bowl of food in front of me and I sit up straight. It's Avery L and she gives me a smile and then… "Look out, blondies!" I hear Samantha call which wakes up Louis and Kelsey who stand up, catching two water bottles that were sailing towards them. Samantha casually places a bottle down for me and Cloud normally.

"Don't call us that." Louis and Kelsey grump at which Samantha just laughs. I take a bite of food and turn my head to look at the Guards. They're all sitting around too. It's rare that we all go a morning without a daily, morning 'pep talk' which is just Sebastian and Rain taunting us, then us being ordered to train.

This all feels strange and I decide that I can't take the anxiety this is causing me and stand up. "Sit down." I hear Ricky say. "No." I say under my breath, fists curled.

"I said sit down. This is your second warning, shortcake."

I say nothing and I hear Ricky stand. "Do you want me to fetch the leaders? Cause I will."

"Haha, don't make me laugh! You don't got the guts for that. I know you're just some softie on the inside, Ricky and you're just as much as scared of them as we all are. I also know about your little 'thing' with Samantha." I taunt.

"Oh, why you little..." Ricky grumbles. I hear Samantha slam her fist, standing up and walking away from the table angrily. "Valerie, what has gotten into you this morning? This isn't you!" Avery pleads, standing up and taking my arm to which I turn around and push her to the ground.

"Ow! Valerie!" She cries with tears in her eyes. "I know all about your thing too with Shelby, so don't try. Question is... What else do I know?" I say, crossing my arms and glaring at the Guards.

"What is up with you? You've been behaving weirdly... But I have no doubt something is going on to cause you to aft out. Is their anything you want to know? If so, ask anything you like. You've proved your worth." Paige speaks up, intervening on behalf of Ricky. For a second, her face softens. "But reme mber...

The people is this room might be who you need to fall on when times get tough, Valerie. Push them away and you'll fall...

We all know the leaders are bullies enough as it is, so please don't start down that path!" She warns, tears almost filling her eyes. "Valerie...." Kelsey trails off looking at me shocked with Louis and Cloud. I slowly sink to my seat. What am I doing? This isn't me...

"W-where are the Lead-" but I don't get to finish.

"Right here, Sprout."

I flinch upon hearing an unexpected voice. "Seems someone woke up on the wrong side of the bed this morning." I hear Rain taunt.

Sebastian and Rain stop in front of the cafeteria. "You got guts this morning, Valerie. Can't say I'm too impressed that you're pushing your fellow comrades around. Our Guards are one thing, hehe." Sebastian says. "But..." He trails off.

"What's that supposed to mean?!" Kelsey yells standing up. "Sit her down!" Rain yells to which Paige forcing Kelsey to sit down by pressing on her shoulders. She yelps in pain. Sebastian cracks a toothy grin.

"I must say, you Guards are pathetic if you can't deal with one rebellious competitor community member, geez!" Sebastian grumbles.

"Right, food & water and then do whatever you want under the watchful eye of our Guards. Training is canceled and for the rest of you, work is suspended." Sebastian says, walking off alongside Rain.

"What...?" I whisper, gently standing up. I've had enough of everything! "Hey!" I yell going to run after them, but Paige stands in my way.

"What?" Sebastian grumbles, turning around, his arms crossed. "You would never let any of us off so easily, any day of the week. What are you up too?" I challenge. Sebastian jumps back a bit, not expecting my words.

"What is up with ME?! You don't have the audacity or right to ask and know the answer! What is up with you, hmm?" He challenges back. I just glare.

"Cute, real cute. Alright, I'll play, but I will level the playing field, you hear me, Valerie? Now go sit or I will make your regret it. Go back to bed if you have too, provided it brings fourth an attitude change." Sebastian says walking off.

"Sebastian, come on. We gotta keep searching for her." Rain whispers, signalling to him. Her?

"You mean, Shelby...?" I ask and both Shelby and Rain both turn around in shock. "Right, it seems you are not going to stop being a thorn in my side today!" Sebastian says loudly. "What do you know?"

I shrug. "Tell me!" He yells, gripping me by collar and lifting me up off the snow covered ground. I gulp. "That's what I thought, Valerie." And he throws me to the ground. I cry out in pain a little.

"Another Angel!" I cry. "WHAT. DID. YOU. SAY?!" He yells. "Another Angel!" I say again, cowering. "I don't believe you, Valerie. She doesn't know any other Angels, but ie. What, is the cold air getting into your head?" He mumbles, turning away.

"I'm telling the truth!" I cry. "Sure, you are." Rain responds sarcastically.

"Please, you have to belie-" but I don't get to finish as I feel Sebastian's boot come into contact with my ribs and I scream in pain, curling into a ball, shaking.

"Well, that shut you up. Next time, don't. tell lies." Sebastian says, walking away and then my vision darkens as I pass out, but not before seeing my friends bend down to me, but no words come from their lips as I watch them speak.

I groan, trying to roll over, but it's not easy. I can feel a pillow under my head. I slowly open my eyes seeing I'm on some kind of camper bed in a white tent. I sit up, but quickly fall down feeling pain.

"Did that teach you not to anger the leaders when they are already pissed off?"

I look and see a woman I've never seen before. "You're not a Guard..." I whisper. "You're right, I'm not. My name is London, Doctor."

I nod. "Good." She says, standing up. "Your ribs aren't broken, luckily. I will tell you, you know it could have been so much worse for you if Sebastian wasn't preoccupied. If He had used more force, you might have needed minor, emergency surgery."

"And I'd die..." I trail off. "What? Oh, no, no! Owen would perform it. I don't like doing surgery and in some circumstances
Sebastian does, but not that often.

He doesn't care for us as much." She trails off. "And, I heard
you upset Ricky and Sam! For what it's worth, the Guards all
still really care about her, you know?

Anyway, get out of here. You can go! And if you feel like
you're having trouble breathing or any symptom that scares
you... Uh, call for a Guard." She offers me her hand, quickly
shakes mine and retracts hers.

I stand up, wobbly on my feet, but leave the tent, seeing
a red medical plus symbol on the tent as I exit it. When I
step out, the sky is a dark blue and the stars are out. The
temperature has dropped to chilly.

Was I out the whole day?

"Valerie."

I jolt hearing a voice and look up to see Avery. She's rugged
up and has a cup in her hands. "What are you doing here?" I
ask. "Waiting, for you." She responds.

"Listen Avery, I–"

"I understand, Valerie. You don't need to say, 'sorry' At one
point or another... This entire situation were all in gets the
best of us and we snap. Today was that day for you. I must say
though... it could have been much worse for you if Sebastian
and Rain weren't proccupied. So please promise me you'll
never to do that again.

I really care about you and I hope we can be friends!"

She gives me puppy eyes.

I nod. "Listen, um. About what I said about you and Saman tha..."

"My old friendship with Shelby? It's true, we used to be friends, but we quickly fell out of love if you know what I mean. And Yes, I said, 'love', this wasn't just something simple.

Seeing what happened to you today, really scared me, but it's amazing to also see someone so confident who will stand up to the leaders time and time again. You're an impressive and beautiful soul, Valerie."

"Thank you." I respond, looking down. "Are you in pain?" Avery asks, concerned as she approaches me.

"A little, but it will heal..."

"Yes, it will. You're right."

"Do you want to know about, Shelby?" I ask. She nods. "She's in a better place. Another Angel snatched- Well, not snatched." I say.

"You're telling the truth? I'm glad, it will be good for her to get away from here..." She responds.

"You know, you didn't have to wait out in the cold for me to awaken." I tell her.

"I wanted too and... Someone needed to be here for when you awoke. Your yeam and my team are having an ally meet- ing. Come on, I'll show you." She says, starting to walk and I follow.

"Want a sip?"

"What?" I ask confused. "Rain came out here and gave me a cup of hot chocolate. I waited hours in the cold and she actually felt guilty and bad for me. She doesn't want to admit it, but she does have a good side to her, but sadly tries to exchange it in for staying Sebastian's wife.

They fight all the time, like alot. Anyway, have a sip. You're likely hungry and thirsty. We'll get you something proper to eat when were back at the dorms."

I nod and we walk in silence. Avery hands me what's left of the cup. "Valerie."

"Yeah?" I ask, turning my head and I feel a pair of lips on the side of my cheek. Avery smiles at me warmly.

We both turn our heads slightly, trying to hide the blush that's on our cheeks.

"You don't have a boyfriend, right?"

I can see she's internally panicking...

"Uh, no, no. I don't, you don't need to worry about any competition..." I panic too.

"Uh, that's good! Valerie, I care alot about you. You mean the world to me and I like- No, love you."

Chapter 13

We see Samantha's up ahead and so was Kelsey and Louis. We all duck down a side street to talk and Cloud is there with the two guys on Samantha & Avery's team. Everyone seems to be in a bit of a bad mood.

After some time spent talking, it turns our "ally's" have been hiding and stockpiling some stuff for ages. They had planned to leave, taking their chances to go into the frozen wasteland, the odds of survival higher if they're not supply-less and wanted us to come with them.

Turns out too, Samantha being cruel to me was a diversion for the guys on her team to steal a few supplies because the leaders back were turned, but also to prove a point. Namely bully me...

And now they're angry at me for the things I said which is understandable except for Avery. She says that she doesn't blame me for snapping, but I should try and make it up to everyone if I can later.

We hit our rooms quickly, then we leave. It's very easy for us to sneak, or should I say, walk out the main gates actually because security was down due to leaders looking for Shelby.

Samantha said that as long as we don't touch Merge in it's raw form with our bare hands or fall into any lakes, rivers or breath it in, we should be fine. Were geared up, taking the proper precautions.

I don't know where were going, but we can't stay at the Community any longer.

The injury I received was only half the strength so none of us want to see Sebastian's fully capable of. It's why were leaving. The leaders are dangerous, but I can't help feeling that perhaps what were doing is reckless, but staying is also risky!

It's a matter of weighing up the choices and consequences though. It's cold out here and I don't know how far we'll need to walk before we stop and settle down to make a home, but we will need to walk a long distance in case the leaders come after us...

"Do you think there is life out here?" I hear Cloud pipe up. "Maybe, maybe not." Samantha responds.

"Meaning?" Cloud follows with. "We might run into an odd community member out here who escaped like us. That pla ne... It might have been one of them.

No doubt by now that whoever they were will never be getting out of prison or Sebastian's labs, but there won't be a whole civilization if that's what you're expecting."

After that, the whole conversation dies down and we pass lots of frozen trees, hills, lakes and surprisingly, polar bears with their cubs in the distance. By now I'm shaking and I look behind me to see just snowy whiteness for miles around.

"Valerie's cold." I hear Avery speak up. "Are you okay, Valerie?" Cloud asks from behind. I begin to shake more. "Don't worry about me." I lie bitterly, looking away. I hear Louiw and Keleey sigh, approaching me. "Please don't be angry at Us, Jesse. I know that we were all angry at you for how you acted and the things you said, but were all stuck in this world together and eachother is all we have.

You snapped, but your not the first person too. We all have bad qualities and... You and me have had the best relation-ship ever, really..." Kelsey tells me.

"Are you in pain?" Louis asks to which I stammer out a, "Y-Yes."

"Come here." Kelsey says, bending down, allowing me to climb onto Her back. Louis gives my hand a reassuring squeeze. "It will be okay, we'll just walk a bit further and put up a thermal tent we have and continue tomorrow morn-ing light once we've decided where going from here." Louis speaks.

I nod and just curl my arms around Kelsey's neck, shaking as we walk further into the snow as daylight begins to slowly descend into darkness.

What they all didn't know though was five people miles back behind them...

Five snow mobiles are parked and it's riders were all rugged up. One of them was looking around through a pair of binoculars and one of the others was checking a map. "We need to find them. They won't survive out here too long." Says the man looking at the map.

"This is by far, one of the most stupidest things Samantha has ever done!" He adds on.

"Yes. Yes, it it is, Sebastian." Answers Rain, her hair up in a bun, hiding beneath a beanie as she watches her three adopted children muck around in the snow together, playing. Come on, children. Back on. We have to find them before tomorrow." Sebastian announces.

"We won't survive either unless we don't set up a shelter now." Responds Owen and they all start setting up a shelter for the night, Harriet & Shelby actually working together.

Four and a half hours later, it's dark out and just as were about to stop and pitch our tents, I feel myself sinking slowly as I was becoming too much for Kelsey that she was hunching over now, but she insisted on still carrying me.

While she slows down, I see a small cabin in the distance.

"Look, over there!" I hear Cloud call and we all start running over to it as the snow storm were in, picks up, snow squelching beneath our boots.

Samantha & Avery with the help of the two guys on their Team pull the door open and move aside letting Kelsey in first to carry me inside, followed by Cloud dragging an exhausted Louis inside and then they all follow, pulling the door shut.

It's not very big and quiet bare except for a couch with a spring or two poking out, an upturned cardboard box table with some folding chairs, small kitchen and I see one single bed in the corner and Kelsey carries me over to it, laying me down gently before she slumps to the floor, groaning which scares the geebies out of Louis.

I wake up a few hours later feeling a gentle warmth. Opening my eyes and then sitting up to see Samantha and Louis are crowded around a fireplace, eating some bread with jam on it.

Kelsey is looking through a cupboard with Cloud while Avery is just sitting, resting against the wall, nearest to me. The other two guys of there team are also doing the same as her.

"Hi." I speak up, yawning. "Hey, Valerie!" Kelsey calls, still looking through the chest with Cloud. "Want some food?

Louis offers I nod and he prepares me some bread with jam. "So... what's the plan?" I ask.

"Honestly, I never completely thought it through beyond escaping..." Samantha trails off. "But! Our best bet is stay in this small cabin for a little while longer and when it's daylight we go back out there because it will be a bit warm despite the snow and keep walking as far as we can go, but not super late that it becomes night.

We find a cave or somewhere fairly hidden where we won't ever be found and make a home there and live out the rest of our remaining years, complete with our own sustainable farm and everything like that.

It's all sappy I know, but I just wanted to be free. I didn't feel able to withstand a second longer of just being controlled by Sebastian..."

"You don't need to explain why, Sam. We understand." Louis tells her.

"Thank you..." Samantha trails off. She's reserved, but has a good soul. "There's food for everyone else!" Louis speaks up, holding a stack more pieces of bread with jam. Kelsey & Cloud stop for a moment to take a bite.

Avery and the other Guys are still asleep. "Let them rest, they deserve it." Louis says, knowing what I was thinking. "If you want me to take over Sam so you can have a sleep like the rest of your team, go ahead." Louis suggests.

"Y-you sure? I-I never usually rest... I-I always worry about them and..." She trails off bringing her hands to her chest. Louis nods. "Yes, you deserve it too. I don't think you and Valerie are that different from eachother. You both look out for everyone else and never take a moment for yourself.

Isn't that right, Valerie?" Louis says looking at me.

"Y-you think of me like that? I act nothing like that!" I choke out. "What? Of course you do. You would spend time with and helper younger kids who were new the teachings of magic and in sports, you were often team leader." He smiles.

"O-okay, maybe only five minutes..." She trails off, curling up on the floor near Avery. Soon she starts to snore slightly and the only ones of us, awake now is me, Louis, Kelsey and Cloid "Just us now..." Louis point out.

-

--

"That was so good!" Kelsey squeals.

"Yes, it was nice to have an uninterrupted meal. Good thing too is that Valerie has no one taking food away from her." Cloud comments. "Yeah, you're right! Finally now, she might gain some weight back and some strength." Louis says in agreement.

"So, who did you thinks lives here?" Cloud questions. "Dunno, but we might wanna leave as soon as possible. Who knows when or *if* the potential occupant will come back and I don't think they will be happy to find a group of strangers in their house." Louis says. "We leave at first light then." Kelsey adds on.

It's nice to see all my friends getting along. It's been ages since we have. All we have been doing is fighting with eachother. They all deserve this block of peace too. Not just me and Samantha!

They all have done so much for me the past few weeks and carried me when I could no longer carry myself. "So, found anything good in the cupboard?" I ask. "Not much, random stuff." Cloud replies back. "You will make sure not to disturb it's contents too much, right?" Louis asks looking unhappy. "Sure, we will! Don't worry!" Kelsey responds in a cheeky manner. Her and Cloud look at eachother, smiling. "Okay... If you're sure." Louis replies, looking unsure.

After this, the conversation dies down and my friends all hit the hay as well. Guess it means I should go back to sleep too... I can't help this feeling that is at the back of my gut, telling me that something is wrong here. I stand up, slightly wobbling to look out the window.

The sky is a light blue with minor purple hues despite it being night time. Almost as if it was day, but it's not. I guess that night's here are pretty different compared to back home, huh? None the less, it's beautiful! Beautiful beyond belief! I look at the the massive forest of trees around us that are decorated in snow.

So frail they are, but they glisten in the light of the moon. Even the lakes and ribers with Merge all frozen around the edges look beautiful, the water has a purple tinge to it at night.

Very different from when we spent hours walking past them earlier when it was daylight. You can't argue that none of this is beautiful, despite it being dangerous, but beauty is dangerous, hehe! I sigh and rest my head on my arms as I just stare out. I don't mind the slight chilly breeze that's lingering as the fire is still on, warming up the room. My hair blows ever so gently with the small bubbles of wind there is.

I wake up later slightly confused. Did I fall asleep at the window? I stand up straight from leaning on the window ledge to see the night is getting lighter, but it's still "dark" out. The room feels slightly cold though...

I take a look at the fire seeing that it has run out of wood. It's not too cold, but eh. Should I wake someone so I can light the fireplace again? or I should let the person I choose have their sleep, uninterrupted? I decide against waking anyone and feel more awake just wanting to stare out the window again at the world. I can see far away on the hills is a mom polar bear and her cubs, playing in the snow. It's so adorable!

Just then I see the light shift a bit and a gentle aura appears above the hills in different tones. It's an aurora! It's so beautiful! I look behind seeing everyone is asleep. I shouldn't wake them, but I wish they all could get a chance to see it. Maybe another night they will? Just then I hear a ticking and look to see a clock near Cloud is making a bit of sound, the hand slowly moving towards 5 a.m o it. I'll wake them all up soon so we can hit the 'road' again.

Just then I hear a strange sound. It's like the whir of a motor...? I lean out the window as I best I can despite my short height to look around. I can see blocky shapes in the distance with what looks like people ontop. Bright lights are shining at the front...? Oh no!

I step back shaking a bit. I going to feel so guilty for this! I bend down, shaking Louis awake by his collar. "Louis, wake up!" I cry. "Huh? W-what's wrong, Valerie?" He asks groggy. Kelsey and Cloud sit up too, hearing my panic followed by both the Guys of Avery and Samantha's team plus them, themselves.

"What's the matter?" Samantha asks, standing up, holding her back like it hurts, but they did sleep on a hard wood floor while I had a proper bed while Louis and Kelsey slept on the couch and Cloud sleeping on some foot ottmans.

"Valerie, babe, you okay?" Avery asks me, standing up as well.

"Huh, it's pretty much daylight." I hear Louis comment, rubbing his sore, tired eyes. "It wasn't the best sleep, but it was something." Kelsey comments..

"We need to go, now!" I cry pointing out the window. "What is that sound?" Sam asks, walking over to the window and Avery passes her a pair of binoculars so she can look further into the snow. Her face literally drops as she slowly lowers the binoculars, hands shaking.

"Crap!" She curses under her breath and I feel her shove me out the door into the snow that I almost trip. She puts the binoculars away into her backpack, slinging it onto her back. "We gotta go, now!" She yells, running out and grabbing my hand, to pull me along.

I look back seeing the panic stricken faces of everyone as they grab their stuff too. I see Cloud open the cupboard quickly and I see him pull out an exact replica of a Core control panel. Oh my god... He quickly hides it in his back-pack. Did he find it, steal it? Is he going to make us go home later?

We all start bolting through the snow. "If we can get lost in the snow, they will lose sight of us!" Samantha exclaims, grabbing onto my wrist to increase my speed as we all run, our feet sinking into the snow. It's fresh. It must have snowed again overnight.

Just then I hear the sound of engines speeding up, just gliding across the snow, effortlessly. The Guys and Avery look back as we run. "Is it who we think it is?!" Samantha calls out. "Oh yeah, it is! We might wanna pick up the pace a bit!" Avery calls back and we all start pushing our legs faster. Samantha is still holding onto me. I hear Cloud puffing.

"I am not made for this anymore! I'm much older than all of you! My broken body and aching bones!" He complains.

"Yeah, yeah, yeah, I get it, Grandpa! But we don't have time to stop now!" Samantha says harshly back. I see a river ahead of us that it frozen over, but it's quite large and will be difficult for us to all run across. Unless we all can leap onto it perfectly and somehow glide over wearing our shoes, then... "Are we goanna able to make it across there?!" I call out. "Oh, yikes! I see what you mean!" Louis responds back.

"We're just goanna have too..." Samantha says shortly. "My cousins right, we don't got much of a choice!" Avery responds back. Were nearing the frozen river and then I just hear this *

whoomp* sound and I hear the sound of something being launched. A pile of snow fly's up near the Guys, but just missing them to which they gasp and speed up again.

"Seriously?! They have what ever that was to launch out of something like a canon?! Argh! You have gotta be kidding me!" I hear Kelsey complain.

"This is not good! This is not good!" I hear Avery saying repeatedly. "Hello, more running, less talking!" Samantha grumps, still holding my hand.

I hear the sound of something being launched again and this time it lands near Avery, but just missing her. "Let's hope they don't figure out how to aim properly!" Cloud calls out.

"Were less than half a meter to the river!" Samantha calls out pointing, we push our selves more and Louis followed by Kelsey race across, slightly slipping, but manage, getting to the other side in one piece. Cloud goes afterwards. "Weeeeeeeee! That was actually fun!" I hear him say.

"Come on, you can do it!" They all call. It's just me, Samantha, Avery and the Guys who haven't crossed yet. Samantha looks back quickly as she pulls me along. "Ah, fudge it!" I hear her say and she roughly grips me back. "What are you doing?!" I cry out. "Helping you! What does it look like?!" She yells back and she gives me a good throw forwards a bit more so that I'm ahead of her, Avery and the Guys.

"Valerie, come on!" Kelsey calls out and I see her, Louis and Cloud are spread out on the other side to catch me when I finish sliding so I don't fall into the snow, wasting precious seconds. Just then I hear the Guys scream and I see them hit by a net, knocking them down together, wrapping around them both, that they can't get up. "Just run, Avery!" They both shout.

"You're almost there!" Louis calls out, his arms open to catch me. I hear the sound of what sounds like a megaphone. "If you three cross that river at the same time, it could break under your feet!"

"That's the chance we're all goanna take, Sebastian!" Avery calls back. I quickly look back seeing that Hariet, Shelby and Owen have stopped to grab the Guys. It's just Rain and

Sebastian who are proceeding. "No, stop! It's too risky!" I hear Rain try also, but we ignore her. "God, don't you know when to listen! Stop, this instant!" Sebastian commands again.

I reach the frozen river and I put my feet on an angle getting ready to slide across and I feel a force behind my back pushing me that I'm given an extra boost, it was Avery! I start gliding across, but it's so slippery that my body is going really fast and my friends are running which ever way, struggling to predict where I could end up so I don't fall flat on my face.

"Stop!" I hear Sebastian yell. I'm almost to the end and I see Samantha grab Avery roughly, throwing her just like she did with me, but Sebastian and Rain jump off their snowmobiles, running towards them.

"Oh no, you don't, Sprouts!" Sebastian yells, fighting with Samantha who has yet to cross. Avery has pretty much only just made it onto the ice and Rain leans forwards, grabbing her arm.

"You are not going anywhere, Avery!" She hisses and Avery starts straining to pull out of her grip.

"No! Let go of me!" She cries out trying to fight Rain. "Rain, get off the ice, god-damn it!" Sebastian yells at her which gives Avery a chance to break out of Rain's grip and Avery throws herself stomach first on the ice, sliding across at an impeccable rate. Wow! Just then I hit the end of the frozen river, almost tumbling with force and Louis grabs onto me last minute. "Got you!" He smiles, pulling me into a hug. Kelsey and Cloud come close to us. "I think we should RUN!" Cloud yells.

"Uh, duh! We got Valerie and that's all that matters!" Kelsey yells, pushing Cloud and they start running. Louis grabs onto my coat, pushing me forward. "Just run!" He yells and I bolt then Kelsey grabs onto me, pushing me that I end up in distance with Cloud while she's behind us.

"What is that Blondie doing?!" Cloud yells. "Staying back for Avery?!" Kelsey responds. "Louis, forget her!" Kelsey yells back. I'm shocked to see his staying.v

"I'm sorry, but I can't!" Louis calls back who is still standing at the edge of the frozen river, waiting to catch Avery

"Got you!" I hear Louis say and he pulls her up off the ground, dragging her along behind Kelsey, I & Cloud.

What a bad time for, 'No one left behind', Avery and Louis quickly catch up to us putting distance between us and the river. I hear Rain raging that we escaped and we all look back seeing Samantha land a sock on Sebastian to his nose and she just sprints across the river, absolutely booking it! "Yes! Sam!" Avery cheers as she runs, her arms in the air.

"The time for celebration can be later!" Cloud yells to which Avery shuts her mouth instantly. Just then a mighty crack rings out and I see Samantha slip, falling into the river, but she pulls Her self out quickly. "Shit..." I hear Avery whisper and then we run and run till we end up in a clearing of trees, but the mountain range goes in a circle that there is no way out.

We stop to quickly catch our breath. "Are you okay, Valerie?" Kelsey says, approaching me and wrapping me in a hug. I nod, intensely. "Good." She responds shortly.

Avery is coughing pretty hard and Louis is pretty much hitting her back to help her. Cloud's still on 'flight' Mode. We see Samantha approach us, dripping wet and dragging her feet.

Her clothes are drenched, eyes red and filled with tears.

"Sam!" Avery cries, running up to her, but Cloud prevents her, dragging her back. Sam's standing there, shivering and wraps her arms around herself, her teeth chattering

"A-are you sick?" Louis asks. Samantha just closes her eyes, continuing to shake.

"Sam!" Avery cries out again, trying to pull herself from Cloud's grip, but he doesn't let go of her. Samantha opens her eyes a second later, letting out a shaky breath. "Ju-just go." She chokes out and we look at the mountain range behind us. "None of us are climbers. Were not trained professionals and don't have the experience." Louis warns.

"Oh so, you wanna wait for Sebastian and Rain to catch up to us, huh?" Kelsey scolds walking towards it and putting Her foot on one of the rocks and her hands up higher. "You coming, Valerie." She calls back, looking at me.

"Come on this is risky, Kelsey. We shouldn't do this!" Louis pleads. "What if one of us fell and broken our neck from a great distance or our back. We'd survive, but be paralyzed or even die."

"And we have no where else to go Louis, but up!" She argues back. I go to step forward towards Petra, but Louis seizes my shoulders. "No, we'll find another way." He says.

"We don't have time for this!" Samantha finally speaks. I see Cloud shrug and he pushes Avery towards Kelsey who takes her hand, pulling her up the first 'step' so she's on the mountain cliff too. "Valerie?" I hear Nell saying in a scared tone. Petra is nodding her head for me to keep climbing.

Louis looks back to Samantha. "I-I can't go w-with you all." She chokes out, shaking more. "It's the e-end of t-the r-road f-for me. G-good luck, Avery. I-I b-believe in you." And Samantha has the biggest smile on her face as she gazes at Avery. "I'll miss you, Sam!" Avery says.

"I know, and I will miss you too. I love you." Samantha smiles, her lips turning blue. Louis looks sympathetic.

"I'm staying with Sam so she isn't alone."

"Stay safe, Louis..." Kelsey says, looking like she's about to cry. "Yeah, you to. All of you."

We leave him behind with Samantha. His made his decision.

"That girl is going to die." I hear Cloud say under his breath. "Why?" Kelsey whispers back.

"That was frozen water. There was Merge in it's raw form in it." Cloud answers. Avery doesn't seem to be hearing a word of this as she keeps climbing. As we climb, Louis with Samantha gets smaller and smaller, I look up seeing the sky going dark.

"What's happening?!" I hear Avery panic. "I-I don't know! It shouldn't be night yet... My guess though is this is our magical 'friends' doing..." Cloud trails off as we keep climbing towards the top of the mountain range. The aurora and stars coming out to say, 'hello' again now.

Chapter 14

The snow storms lightly falling and decorating me and my friends as we all lay there in the middle of the snow under a withered tree that's offering us no protection. The snow flurries that are falling around us are beautiful, no two snowflakes the same, just spinning and glittering in the process.

I take a breath out, watching my cold breath mix with the frozen air once it leaves the safety of my mouth. I turn my head ever so slightly to gaze upon Kelsey body and face that is close to mine, her hair is outspread, no longer in two pigtails and her lips blue are blue too, eyes big and dulled, fingers barely moving and she's decorated by snowflakes along the layer of her clothing.

I look a few steps away from us at Avery and Cloud. They are in the same position as us, decorated by snow flurries, but are so much further gone than me and Kelsey.

Their skin is silver and their lips bright blue, eyes closed, but their chests rising and fallen every few seconds to indicate their last fleeting seconds upon them.

Were all going to die out here. It won't be much longer and then we can just all drift away into the frozen oblivion of the cold together.

"V-Valerie..." Kelsey whispers next to me, trying to roll over and lean on my shoulder. We grasp each-others hand, fingers locking, but shaking still from the cold. She rests her head on my shoulder.

"T-the t-temperature is d-dropping."

"I-I know. It's dark out too and I-I don't know why. Why did this have to be w-where we e-ended up?"

"At l-least were together."

"Y-yes, we are.

"Valerie, I-I know y-you think were not friends, b-but I wanted you to know that I consider you a friend and I look up to you too. You're a role model for s-so many p-people.

A highlighter in the darkness."

"You think that of me?"

"I-I do."

"I've been jealous of you, Kelsey. It's hard t-to explain out here, but I want you to know that I d-don't hate you.

It's going to be over for us soon and w-we can drift away into oblivion's together, friend."

"W-what? I-I don't understand..."

"I'm in love with Louis."

She doesn't answer me. "Kelsey!" I cry out, seeing her eyes drop closed.

"Kelsey! Wake u-up, please!" I manage to cry again, unable to move from the cold to try and wake her up again. I feel tears run down my cheeks.

Her chest is falling and rising only now. It won't be much longer for me now. I lean my head slightly next to hers, just staring up at the snow falling. The aurora is out, it's beautiful.

You can can see a single moon and it has a silver outline around it, but the center a faded black. It's all truly beautiful this world, but also deadly.

I don't want us to die here, I don't want to die here, but there's nothing I can do and no one's out here, but us.

No one's going to be able save us either. Not even a good. So much for Kiki.

It's time I accepted my fate and I breathe out one final breath and let my eye lids close feeling the snow flurry land upon them, gently. I feel myself drifting away to be ready to let my soul depart from my body and this world, but without knowing why. I snap and try one last minute ditch attempt to survive and I cry out out for anyone, someone to help us.

Anyone, someone to help me, eyes still closed. I don't give up ever and fight to the end so maybe that is why...

"Help, somebody help us, please! Were going to die out here and it's cold! Two of my friends have been out for hours and Kelsey just fell asleep! I'm the last one left!

"Valerie Woods!"

My eyes snap open, all my senses being flooded. I see a bright white light above me and a blue butterfly is floating there.

"It's okay, reach for me."

I try to move my arm to raise it, but it feels stiff and I can't. Sitting up is also impossible.

"You can do this, Valerie. I know you can, you're stronger than you realize. You gave up once so don't make the same mistake twice in giving up!"

"W-who are you?" I ask.

The voice doesn't respond and then I feel light-headed, weight-less. I see I managed to raise my arm up to extend it towards the butterfly, but I realize my arm is ghostly and my real arm is still stuck beside my body.

"Valerie, come to me, please! You know me! Don't give up, there is morr than meets the eye here!" The voice begs. I grit my teeth and manage to touch the edge of the butterfly's wings. They're soft and the light explodes, the butterfly apart of it.

As I lay there, breathing differently, I feel like I can breathe easily, like my powers are flowing through

I see the world around me glitch out slightly by fading or pulsing and there is coloured crack-like shapes.

I see my friends are fading in and out with the world. Then it hits me. I gulp. Multiple outcomes. For some reason I'm shifting between the possible realities of this world.

If I'm hopping, how do I stop? If I manage to stay in one, what happens to me? I don't know enough about this and fate changing, our destiny's, is it noticeable to my friends or just to me?!

Then I hear a cracking sound and the world halts from changing.

"You're looking a little cold right there, Sprout."

No..."S-Sebastian! I choke out and my chest heaving in pain to see him standing there, wrapped up in a purple coat, but his blurry.

"Are you doing this?" I ask.

"Doing what?" He responds puzzled. Either his lying and playing dumb or he must not be affected by what I'm going through, but how? He and his wife are so superior to me...

He chuckles, smirking at me. "K-Kelsey! Help her! S-she's out, she passed out!" I cry, blinking back tears to see Kelsey has re-appeared.

I see him nod and I see Rain appears wrapped up in a white coat and approaches Kelsey, placing her arm behind her back, bringing her into a sitting position and pulls out a coat for her from nowhere, then wraps a scarf around her neck and slides a beanie over her flyaway, loose blonde hair.

She then walks out of sight with her.

"W-where are you taking her?!" I choke out, but Sebastian just smirks at me, saying nothing and I see they have back-up. I didn't see them with back-up earlier. Ricky carries Cloud and Paige carries Avery.

"Are they alive?" I beg, straining.

"Their pulse is low, breathing shallow, but they're alive." Paige answers.

Sebastian fobs her off with a hand signal. I watch as he bends down on his knee close to me and brings his hand out, stroking and playing with my raven hair, messing it up a bit for a few seconds. His eyes looking longingly, but he says nothing.

I turn my head away from him, but his hand firmly grips the side of my chin, forcing me to look at him again and he folds his arms to rest on his knees. I spit at him and he wipes it off with his sleeve, only slight annoyance on his race

"You are not in the position to be making demands, Valerie. Let me tell you something. I always win."

I watch him reach into his coat pocket and he pulls something out. A sharp needle and it's full with a pale pink liquid and rests it on his lap.

"Now let me tell you something, Sprout. I could just leave you out here in this snow storm. Your body is not going to last much longer and just take your friends and my family back to the community alone without you or I could inject you, knocking you out so you are 'co-operative' back with your Friends to the community.

What's it gonna be?"

I grit my teeth, thinking it over. Do I want to die out here, standing up for what I believe in or give in and live to see another day?

"W-what will y-you do to m-me if I come back with y-you?"

"Don't know. Say yes and find out."

"But how will I know if you will keep your word?"

"I guess you'll just have to find out, Valerie. You can say, 'no' if you don't trust me or trust me and find out if I keep my word. It's your choice, Sprout.*

I blink tears away from my eyes and I see him stand up away from me. "You're taking too long to choose. I hope your 'happy and content' with your decision." He says walking away to get back on his snow mobile and placing the needle away.

"W-wait!" I cry out, willing myself to move through the thick, cold layer of snow that I fall onto my stomach, crawling on all fours towards him. He climbs off his snow mobile, clapping his hands.

"There we go! Just what I wanted to see. Now you are playing MY game. You're a natural and perfect for other plans too! You have a fighting spirit despite thinking you don't possess one."

He leans down to me, roughly pulling me onto my feet, but then pushes me down that I fall flat on my back in the snow again. "Do you want us to put her in the back of the truck with the rest?" I hear Ricky ask, walking over to Sebastian.

"Nah, this one's mine. Lock it up and move out." He says and Ricky nods, leaving.

"Well, Valerie. It's time to find out if I keep my word." He says, walking over and roughly gripping my arm, pulling my sleeve up that my arm is exposed and presses the needle down, then pulls it out.

I feel him pull my sleeve down and lift me up. This could be worse... He could have sedated me and left me in the snow and I feel him place me on the front of his snow mobile and he takes a seat behind me, placing his arms on either side of me to grip the handle bars of the snow mobile. There is a lack of space between us.

"Keep your legs up while I drive." I hear him caution or should I say, 'order' and I place them on the space available where you put your feet. It's cold and he hasn't given me a coat or anything like they gave Kelsey or the rest of my friends.

I feel the snow mobile start up and we start driving, snow flying everywhere as we take off back towards, 'home".

They should have just thrown me in with my friends, but I guess they wanted me to suffer a bit and so that Sebastian could keep a close, personal eye on me. Creep.

Chapter 15

I look at the IV, unsure what is going into me and I rip them out despite the pain, not trusting what could be inside them, contents of them slowly dripping onto the floor. I swing my feet the floor, holding onto the bed so I don't fall as I'm standing upright. I take a few steps and stop , seeing another bed like the one I was on, sheets messed up, but tubes empty and a heart monitor. It shows a 'flat-line' symbol...

That makes me nervous! I need to go out of here! I walk to the door and put my hand on the door handle, praying that it's not locked and to my surprise, it swings open. Great! I start bolting the corridor, desperate to get out of wherever here is! I need to find my friends!

Soon enough, I leave behind the cold, white starkness and end up back within the normal hallway that Rain once led me down when we shared a "moment" together over food and drink. So, I'm in the leaders home. I pick up the pace and run across the doorway of the kitchen, seeing the exit door.

"Stop!"

I flinch, freezing hearing a voice and slowly look back "R-Rain...?"

"I see you're awake. You can go. I really don't care, you little shit. All the trouble you caused us to find you and your friends out there in that wasteland. I honestly don't know if was even worth it, but my Husband insisted that we freaking looking for you. He claimed you were worth it and I sure as hell, hope you are worth it, because if turns out you aren't Valerie, well! When I'm done with you, you will wish that you hadn't wished for someone, us to save your sorry ass.

Now leave and go back to the city if you so desire. When I see Sebastian, I will tell him you left and didn't want anymore healthcare." She snaps and saying in an annoyed tone, then taking a sip of something in a coffee cup, still rugged up warmly.

I nod and press the door so I can leave, heading out back into the cold, but safety of the village.

I walk for a little while heading back into the city centre. I need to change because it's cold! Take a quick detour to my sleeping quarters, I gulp when I go in, seeing the beds are stripped of blankets and pillows that only the mattress' are left behind. I check the beside tables seeing our few things that belong to us is gone and I pull open the cupboard relieved to see a few changes of clothes are left.

The leaders must have had the guards clear most of our stuff out, thinking that we wouldn't be coming back at all or if we did, it would be in a body bag... I wonder if Samantha's room is the same?

Shrugging and taking a spare set of clothes to change into and folding the hospital gown up, I close the door, head out to go to the cafeteria. I stumble though halfway through the hall, needing to steady myself.

I feel dizzy... But I push myself on and see the world glitch out again. What's going on?! When I arrive at the cafeteria I see other members eating and the Guards are actually on their feet, cooking. Why does it feel like the room has a different vibe than usual?

"Valerie!"

I turn my head to see who called my name. The two Guys from Samantha team is at my table and Louis is there, waving. "Louis" I scream running over and he leaps to his feet to meet me half-way.

"I was so worried about you!" I cry. "And I am so glad to see you are okay!" He responds back and we embrace, his holds me tight then I hear audibly gasp.

He looks panic stricken and I see the hues and ghostly image a blue butterfly right over his chest. It fades a moment later.

"Louis?" I whisper. He is looking at me intensely despite his wide eyed glossy look on his face. "Are you okay?" I ask.

"Uh... Yeah. I'm... Just so glad to have you back!" He finally speaks after a minute. Taking my hand, he helps me to the table and I sit down, leaning on him and he wraps his arms around me holding me really close as if his afraid I'll melt.

"So, what happened?" I ask then I see the world around me glitch again and his expression looks ever more panicked now for some reason. If I told anyone about the world around me glitching, I wouldn't be believed... I'd be written off as crazy.

"I spent a few days in recovery with these guys and then I was just sent back to the city. We've been staying in a spare room somewhere else as our room and Sam's teams rooms have been stripped. Sebastian did come and taunt us saying they found you, Avery, Kelsey and Cloud, but I wasn't sure if it was true.

Ah, I'm so glad you are okay, Valerie!"

But the way he says it feels off and his breathing heavily as if his trying to catch his breath. It's like his not meaning what he says, but I push my feelings aside.

"I was too. I was worried about you, Lukas. Where's Sam and everyone else?"

"You haven't seen them? Oh, geez...This doesn't look good. As for Sam? She was taken for surgery/ I think? I'm not sure.

While I was in a drug induced sleep, I heard yelling about someone going into cardiac arrest, but the Guys were in the room with me so it wasn't them.

T-that's all I know, sorry. Look, we will find the rest of our friends, uh, okay? I promise. I just need... Time to come to terms with all this." He finishes with, hugging me. "This?" I ask, but he shrugs, looking around the room.

One of the Guys standing up walking over to near the guards. "D-do you t-think we c-c have f-food? P-please?"

I see Ricky there who is spinning a loaf of bread around, fresh out the oven. "F-fine, short-stack." He smirks.

"Surprised you're alive, Valerie. Was hoping I wouldn't have to see you again, but here you are and I will destroy you when I get the chance, our name leaders backs turned. You made Emily go out into the snow. She was dear to me and now I don't even know how she is now!" He yells putting the bread and several soup bowls out.

"Help yourselves." He grumbles, walking away and the Guy grabs the food, bringing them to us and we all dig in. After eating for a while, were full and Louis hands me a spare key, telling me where our new shared room is and then I depart to head there while they stay behind to socialize.

After walking for a little bit... I begin to feel lightheaded and I realize that I've sort of just been staggering about, my head is pounding and there is like a fog over my mind and I end up walking into some portal for I don't know what reason. I just know I'm not thinking straight, but my brain doesn't match up with my body.

"Hey, are you okay?"

...

"Hello? Anybody in there?"

I wake up sometime later, dazed and disoriented to see that I'm lying on a single bed in what looks like a shared dorm. I turn my head to see a guy with dark toned skin and brown hair with piercing green eyes who is wearing wearing clothes.

"W-who a-are y-you?" I choke out. He takes a seat on the bed, propping his leg up in his other. "What are you doing here? You're a member from the City. You shouldn't be here unless you made Sebastian mad...

This isn't jail, but this part of the city is typically for exiled people... But people they don't want to let go or lock up."

"I-I don't understand. My head- I feel- I feel..."

"Woah, okay, relax buddy." He says helping me to lie down again and I feel him place a damp cloth on my head. "You're running a fever. What happened to you?" He asks me.

"I went o-out into the c-cold." I choke out. "You went out into the Frozen Wasteland? Wow, you're brave! Let me guess. Did Sebastian drag you back?"

I nod slow and painfully. "I'm sorry this is happening to you. To all the people trapped here. I know Sebastian well because of an incident many years ago.

All of this stuff happening to us is horrible and it will come back to bite him in the rear end hopefully in the future." He says sighing and placing his face in his hands.

"What's wrong?" I ask, leaning forward. "No, don't worry. It's just something from years ago. I haven't seen her in forever and not a day goes by where I don't think of her, worrying about her and if she's okay. I worry that Sebastian hurt her." He says and then he explains a long, complicated story about meeting a girl who was knew to a town and that was really intelligent, then about a android hologram that passed the turing test, a house party with something about strong punch and it took over his home and two mysterious people saved them all from the control of it and then took away someone he loved and he went after them to get her back, then Sebastian had him sent to the poorer districts of this city when they initially asked him to leave and he refused to leave.

"That's an unbelievable story." I tell him. "I know it is. I wish I could see her again. She means the world to me." He explains. "What does she look like? Maybe I've seen her?" I respond and he describes her.

"That sounds just like Harriet!" I tell him, standing up and he jumps up from sitting beside me on the bed I'm in, shaking me. "Y-you've seen her?!" He cries. I nod. "Where is she?! Take me to her! I gotta get her out of here!" He cries.

"D-don't worry, I'll help you." I smile, taking his hand. We head to the edge of the exiled district and see no Guards around. I must have been feeling really off to sleep-walk here or whatever it is I did and I poke my head through, carefully.

"It's clear." I whisper and I sneak him over to the boarding house and unlock the room with the key that Louis gave me and looking for and giving him a change of clothes, scarf and a hat so his less recognizable.

"Thanks, uh... Your name?"

"It's Valerie. And you?" I ask. He looks away. "Don't worry about it." I say.

"Thanks. I'm glad you understand." He responds. "So where is she?" He asks. "In the Leaders house, I think." I respond. We head there and it is surprisingly easy to sneak in. Security really is down in this place at the moment.

We head past the kitchen and I stop slowly seeing Rain's back to us. She's cooking something in a fry pan.

"Is that bacon and egg? Damn, I could really go for a good home-cooked meal at the moment." The Guy behind me asks. I give him a slight slap and and just grab his wrist, heading past Rain as she's distracted. I have him hide and I search all the rooms, getting lucky on one of the last ones. Harriet is inside, doing nothing in particular. She looks sad.

I signal to him and he walks up to me. "You ready?" I ask him. He shakes his head, stepping back. "Hey, come on. We came this far. Go talk to her."

"Valerie, I-I can't!"

"Sure, you can. Just go talk to her."

But he shakes his head and I sigh. "Fine, hide and I'll go talk to Her. She doesn't seem hot-headed like Rain or Sebastian, although she is responsible for us ending up here...."

IHe goes to hide while I place my hand on the door handle, looking back to see him nod. Here I go... And push the door open again and sliding in, closing the door behind me.

"Y-you! You should not be in here!"

I flinch at her sudden anger when she has just been sitting on her bed, starring blankly at the wall. "Hi..." I trail off. "What are you doing in here, Valerie? Be honest with me and I'll let you go and if you don't, I will scream and 'Mum' will come running."

She looks awfully serious. "I-I'm helping someone out." I whisper. "Who?" She says skeptically.

"A guy, he wanted to see you."

I watch Harriet slide off her bed and pull on a sweater along with snow boots and her head-scarf. She looks a bit drugged out. "Is his name, Ethan?" She asks me. I shake my head. "He didn't say. I don't think He trusts me." I respond.

She looks sad. "Why? What's wrong?" I ask, sitting down next to her and gently wrapping my arm around her. She relaxes under my hold and sits down again.

"What's your story, Harriet?" I ask. "Valerie... I... I am so sorry that I pushed you and your friends into this world. I con-demned you Guys to this suffering at the hands of Sebastian I regret doing it." She whispers, tears forming.

"It's okay, don't worry about it. I'm here... to be a hero, a savior if I can be." I smile.

She wipes her eyes with her sleeve, slowly nodding. "I've always asked myself why I wasn't like other girls. I wasn't into fashion or makeup or even talking about boys and I don't always see eye to eye on decision making with Owen, Mum & Dad.

I was into Gaming, Technology. Cliche I know as that is like the number one thing, a girl does when she rebels, but it was me. I had another friend. We got on great, but I slowly ruined it and was horrible to her, but I did because I was dealing with my own demons and I had no way to express the feelings I internally bottled up.

After that, I pretty much just turned to technology as it was something to do and explore compared too what I was going through. I wanted social contact, but something more... I ran away and Dad brought me back 'Home.'

Dad was always so horrible to me and whatever I did was never good enough for him. I tried to assist him, but I was never fast enough or some other arbitrary reason. I tried to be better, but all I did was 'fail' and disappoint him to no end. He hated me and even hurt me. Not just emotionally... I soon grew to learn what he did and he experimented on me once to teach me a lesson do I wouldn't step out of line again and to teach me a lesson.

I'd love nothing more than to leave this place again and never look back with him. Truth is I was in love with him! He was my best friend and maybe he was even more than that?" She says, her face lighting up.

"Harriet..." I whisper not wanting to speak and ruin her train of thought. "Why don't you?"

"What?"

"He's outside, waiting for you, Harriet."

"Y-you mean I c-can s-see him? We can b-be together?!"

I nod, slowly and her face lights up. "Security is low in this place right now and Dad won't expect me to run. W-we can be together and g-go anywhere, together. We can travel and see the w-world! We can go where he will never find us! There are so many worlds out there Valerie each of their own beauty to see."

I watch her grab a small bag, packing stuff like her wallet, a phone, a few clothes, some books and she pulls out a circuit board and some other, but it looks damaged. She fits it in.

"W-what is that?" I ask. "A Friend. She was human despite what she looks like. What happened was an accident, but there's always a chance I can fix her and help Her to better than she was. She wanted the same thing as us! Not to be lonely anymore."

She follows me out the room and when she sees him and he sees her, they embrace and hold each-other, him gently kissing her under the eye. It's beautiful!

"Thank you for everything you have done for me, Valerie. I won't forget this and I know you will be free one day, but right now you will have a fight on your hands. Good luck!" She smiles and then opens her mouth again to speak.

"Come on, let's go!" Harriet says inserting the computer stuff she has into a small looking box and I see a green hologram appear, a girl. She has long green hair, pale skin, dark green eyes, a dark green, somewhat black strapless dress and dark green/black flats. "Harriet, Ethan?" The hologram asks, voice scratchy and slow, albeit confused.

"We'll explain everything later. Just get us out of here right now! Take us anywhere!" Harriet begs and the girl hugs her and Ethan, able to place her arms around them despite being a hologram and they both giggle slightly from her touch. Green electricity all around them and then they are gone, leaving me alone.

Chapter 16

I haven't seen Sebastian, Rain or Owen either and a part of me is curious what they are doing...

Then I hear two familiar voices and slowly look up to see two recognizable bodies, staggering towards us. Tired, drugged, cold and overall, how I feel, but worse as I had 24 hours to kind of wind down during.

The two guys leap up, bringing them to sit down.

"Woah, you guys don't look so crash hot!" Louis points out. "N-no. W-we feel terrible." Kelsey stammers, wrapping Her arms around Herself. Cloud just closes his eyes and rests his head on the table. "Sebastian kicked us out of the infirmary at this home because the hospital was full... We had IV's in us." Cloud says weakly. "Valerie did too, but she left early on, ripping them out... Regardless though, we can't trust them anymore." Louis warns to which we all agree.

He still looks scared, somewhat confused and not meaning what he says. What is up with him?

"What do you think they are g-goanna do to us?" I stammer. "I don't know Valerie, but they are very angry I can tell you that!" Kelsey speaks up, weakly though.

"Hey, let's not worry about anything for the moment if we can and just work on you all getting better... you're all really sick." Louis responds.

"Hey, it's not so bad. Most of us are all together again." One of the Guys say, trailing off. "Have either of you seen Samantha or Avery?" The other Guy asks, prompting Kelsey and Cloud to moan, shaking their heads and plonking them on the table again. Just then I hear voices and look up, gripping Louis. hand. "What's wrong, Marl- Valerie?" He asks me, draping an arm around me.

We all look up, seeing Sebastian, Rain and Owen talking to the Guards. I can faintly make out their conversation. Sebastian is wondering where Harriet has gotten and that she took something "important" and Ricky responds back saying an exiled member is missing, but I'm so sick and tired that I can't concentrate for very long and lean against Louis who his other around me to help keep me upright. After a while the leaders and Guards stop talking and I see Ricky walk over, placing a small vase with a single white flower near the bench where they prepare food...

Everyone on our table stops dead, looking and instantly knowing what it represents. I sware there are tears in his eyes.

I stand up slowly, gripping the edge of the table. "R-Ricky, I-I am so sor-"

"Shut up, Valerie! I don't want to hear it." He growls through gritted teeth. The whole room is silent and staring at us. "No, Ricky. P-please- hear me out-"

"I said enough! It's because of your selfishness, Samantha went out there and she's gone now forever."

I watch his eyes lower and he sits down on his chair, resting his head in hands and the rest of the Guards join him. Everyone else sits down in the room, not saying a word. All I can hear is the gentle howling of the wind and snow flurries. I give up sitting down. "Well, Valerie. That should teach you and your group and everyone else in this room that actions have consequences." Sebastian smirks, walking off with Rain who is smirking and Owen who looks really concerned...

As they leave, I stand up again. "Wait. I have one more question." I whisper and He looks back. "Fine. Spit it out, Sprout."

"Where is Avery?"

"Not where Samantha is right now due to your actions." And then he leaves.

I sit curled up with a pillow in my arms and face resting in it with Kelsey, Cloud, Louis and the two Guys all hanging around in the secret room we found ages ago. We feel so miserable that we just couldn't bear to stay facing the Guards or the other members so we came here to hide.

"I remembered something." Kelsey whispers after some time. "What?" Cloud asks and Louis has just completely shut down on us, hiding next the bookshelf in the corner. He gave his freedom to stay with Samantha to keep her alive, yet it was all in vain. "Just say it, Kelsey." I say in somewhat of a snap even though it's not personal.

She stands up coming over and taking a seat next to me and wrapping her arms around me, resting her head in the crook of my neck and shoulder. "It was your birthday 6 days ago, Valerie. You were out for 8 days... I just remembered. Sorry. I-I know this doesn't make today any better, but, Happy Birthday." She says, giving me a small kiss on my cheek and I just cuddle into her.

"Thanks, Kelsey."

"No problem, Valerie."

We stay together, resting against each-other for the rest of the afternoon. I open my eyes seeing the lights are off, especially outside. Louis, Cloud and the Guys are all asleep, Kelsey is also asleep, just resting still on my shoulder. I wonder how late at night it is?

I flinch hearing footsteps. They sound nearby... no... please don't tell me someone is going to check this room! I leap up, placing my hand on Kelsey's mouth to suffocate her, but I shake Her awake and she opens Her eyes looking shocked, but tired still. I bring my finger to my lips and she nods gently, but quickly standing up to hide behind the couch while I move to Cloud and Louis who also wake up and Louis books it took to wake up the Guys.

We all find a hiding place and quieten our breathing. I hear the sound of wood being wrenched off, and the door being unlocked and a soft light comes in and I hear soft footsteps, coming just a few meters into the room.

...

"I know you, Valerie and your friends are in here."

That voice... It's not Sebastian's, but it's male! I see him turn around and close the door behind him and he locks it from the inside with a key. "You can all come out. I won't hurt you."

I hear a sigh and he starts walking around the room. "It's been a long time since I've been in here here. It used to be my old observatory. I spent many hours, looking into space.

Do you like astronomy, Cloud?"

We all keep quiet and I just hear the man keeping walking around the room, talking about various stuff in the room and his interests.

I hear him take a seat. "I don't blame you Guys for running out into the snow. You're afraid of us and you have every right to be, but out there as beautiful as it is, its also very dangerous.

You all were close to death when we found you. Any longer out there and none of you would have come back here except in a body bag..."

"You're wrong! Were missing one of us." I hear Kelsey call out and I hear the person jump up and then I hear her curse, realizing she gave her location away.

"Shit!" She whispers out and the person is slowly walking around the side of the couch to where Kelsey is. I can't let her be discovered! I leave my hiding place, stepping out. "Hey!" I yell pulling his attention from Kelsey and I see her sneak away to where Cloud is hiding under a table who puts his arm around her.

"Ah, there you are, Valerie."

It's Owen... "H-Hi."

"Don't worry, I won't hurt you. I was doing last minute checks and noticed none of you were in your rooms so I thought I would check some rooms that were hardly used anymore and here you all are. What are you all doing here? Can you all come out?"

I wave my hands and all my Friend stands up. "None of you look so great. You don't need to take my suggestion, but I think you all should perhaps head to bed for the night and rest. Sleeping on the chairs and couches in here won't be comfortable and you won't recover either from going out there in that horrible snow storm."

We all nod. "Head down the hall, turn left, then right and right again and you will find the hallway for the main sleeping quarters."

We all nod. "That's good." He says and we all start leaving. "Don't worry about running into any Guards. They are all in bed, but I highly suggest that you plan *however* you Guys enter and exit this room better. In the mean time, I shall accidentally *misplace* the key."

I follow behind Kelsey when I feel Owen cling onto my arm, stopping me from leaving. "Valerie, you coming?" Owen asks, turning around with everyone. I look at Owen and he seems down?

"Uh, I'll be there soon. Head to bed without me."

"Okayyyyy...." Kelsey trails off leaving with everyone else. After that, the door closes behind us, Owen signals for me to sit and I take a seat, him sitting too. "You okay? You're highly shaken up. What's wrong?"

I look away. "I didn't punish you Guys for being in an off limits area, surely that means I'm trustworthy, yes? I wanted a chance to sit down and talk with you. I know you probably think I have some interesting *friends* but I assure you that we, they weren't always like that, unfortunately time is humanity's worst enemy."

"W-what d-do you m-mean b-by that?" I ask to see him stand up. "You're 100%, positively shaking, Valerie. Umm, do you want to come down to my house? We can talk while I treat you."

I shake my head. "Doctors take an oath to do no harm, Valerie." He says, placing his hands in the pockets of his hoodie. "And Rain said you woke up, leaving instantly.

You're friends stuck around a little longer to get slightly better, but you just took yourself out into the city into the cold which didn't really help you get better."

I slowly nod my head. "Okay, let's go." He smiles, leading me the the door, but on our way, he takes the old coat and scarf in this room we found and hands it to me temporarily for the journey to wear.

I open my eyes slightly still shaking on the bed, Owen has me on and I see him in the corner, slipping a lab coat on, grabbing some stuff and pulling a easily moveable chair over to sit near me. He holds his gloved hand out and I place my arm on him slipping up my sleeve. "I'm just going to take your blood pressure, okay?" He says, wrapping a cuff around it and then marks down blood pressure reading. He listens to my breathing and shines a light in my eyes and some other stuff after a little while.

"Hmm, you're temperature is slowly rising up again to normal, but you're running a slight fever and a little dehydrated. Let me get you some hydralyte" He says, grabbing some for me. I drink it.

He just sits there while I do. "Do you want anything for your fever?" He asks me and I shake my head. "Okay. I won't force you too, but let me do something to help you." He says grabbing a cloth and wetting it then, sliding it onto my forehead. "Does that feel slightly better?"

I nod. "I'm glad, Valerie. You gave us all quite a fright when you and your team went out there, including Samantha's. Why did you Guys do it?"

I look away. "You don't have to tell me, but telling me will help me to understand what happened. You can ask me some questions if you want."

"W-where's Samantha?"

"I'm sorry, but you all ready know the answer to that... Valerie, Merge is a highly toxic in it's raw form. It has sharp barbs and if they pierce your skin, toxic levels of poison are released and that in the blood stream can cause convulsions, fevers and in worst cases... stop your heart and in water, it's a liquid version with slight crystal in it and will poison you much the same.

Now there is an antidote, ironically which involves making it from Merge it's self, but it takes a while and unfortunately there was nothing we could do.

I assure you, Sebastian tried to make an antidote as soon as he could, but time just wasn't our side. He did try to operate too, but as I said, time wasn't on our side."

I nod slowly. "And Avery?"

"She's still recovering. She seems to have been passed out in the cold long before you, Kelsey and Cloud. passed out, but I think she will be fine. I did do minor emergency surgery on her myself, but the end result.,I have no idea if it helped till she wakes up or if she wakes up at all. I won't lie to you."

I nod slowly, feeling tears slip down my cheeks. "W-what were your questions?" I ask slowly feeling myself shake from the cold still. "Ages ago... you said something about Angels... Was what you said was true?"

I nod. "I see. Well, anyway, Harriet has gone missing. Do you know anything about that?"

"I-I'm sorry. I was out of it, I didn't know what I was doing-"

"Don't worry about it, it's fine. If they are together, then I'm happy for her. She never liked this place and I know he will take good car of her. While I'm sad that she's gone and it won't change the feelings I have, as long as she's happy, then her and me will meet each-other again in the future at a truck-stop diner or something. I don't know, life is full of surprises!"

I laugh too at his silly joke. "You feeling slightly better?" He asks me and I nod. "Good, that's good. You should join your friends and get some rest. There's about six hours of night left. It would be better than nothing.

I can take you all off training for a while, but frankly if you ask me, I don't know if Sebastian or Rain will want to see your faces for a while...."

"Okay." I say, sliding to my feet and handing him the wet cloth, but as I grip the door handle to leave. He says something else which surprises me.

"Happy 'belated' birthday, Valerie."

Chapter 17

We haven't seen Avery yet and I ask every time Owen comes around to see us how she is and he says his looking after her and that she's getting better slowly. He comes with our meals and to check each of our health. The Guys from Sam's team have been sleeping on the floor of our room so they didn't have to go back to their team room. I feel bad for them, I really do.

About just after mid-day, I wake up to see my friends are awake and sitting in a circle on the floor, with pillows tucked around them and blankets wrapping around their bodies. The colour has returned to Kelsey's blue eyes which I'm glad. Cloud's hazel eyes too! Louis and the Guy's though were much better than us to begin with, but they are each dealing with emotional demons at night while I, Kelsey and Cloud spend it shivering involuntarily.

Someone knocks on our door.

"I'll get that." Louis says, wearily dragging him-self up off the floor and to the door, his blanket trailing behind him a bit like a robe and pulling the door open to reveal Owen holding a plate full of sandwiches and several cups on it too. "What is in the cups?" Louis asks confused. "Hot Chocolate!" Owen grins handing the plate to Louis who places it gently in the middle of the group. I see everyone reaching for it excitedly. Louis takes a seat as well.

Owen steps into the room, a shoulder bag at his side. "Did she eat or drink yesterday?" He asks.

One of the Guys from Sam & Avery's team, turn to look at me on the bed. "No..." He trails off. Owen walks over to me, kneeling down. He gives my a shoulder a little squeeze. Groaning to look at him, he helps me sit up straight, placing a pillow behind my back.

"Does your stomach hurt?" He asks me to which I whisper a quiet, 'no' and I rub my sore, tired eyes. I feel his hand on my wrists, bringing them down. "Doing that will hurt you." He says gently. "Try and eat something if you can, Valerie" He says with his eyebrows furrowing and me giving him a weak nod. "She's still running a fever." I hear Louis comment to which Owen turns and looks at him.

"You all are." He responds, correcting Louis. "I can give you Guys some medicine. I have it, but you have all been refusing it."

I just groan, laying back a little, closing my eyes. "Hey, come on now, Valerie" He says, sitting me up again, but I don't open my eyes this time. I hear him sigh. "You're not all going to like me, but I think I should give you each a dosage of cold and flu medicine."

I see him looking in his bag and he produces a fine syringe, sticking it into a bottle and pulling it up and out. A second later I feel his firm, but gentle grip around my wrist to stop me pulling away. "This will just be a small pinch, Valerie" And before I know it, his done it and every else, then begs goodbye and leaves us all in peace. After a few minutes, I weakly push my blankets back, standing up, but pretty much falling to the floor which earns a slight gasp from my friends and I crawl over to my Friends. One of the Guys from Sam & Avery's team who helps me sit up straight and I lean on Kelsey who wraps her arm around me.

"W-what are we doing?" I ask. "Just talking." Louis says with a yawn. "About?" I ask. "Anything." Kelsey answers. "We were just talking about our life before we all ended up here and what we would have like to have been doing if we weren't trapped here." Cloud says after her.

"These Guys were just telling us that they are friends and had been on a four day hike when Rain and Sebastian snuck up from nowhere and kidnapped them." Cloud explains to which the Guys agree, nodding. "We saw alot of stuff! We were taking photos of moose's and all kinds of other animals. We even saw an abandoned fire-watch tower and it was near a lake." One of the Guys explain, elbowing his buddy and they both break out in a grin.

"Although, right now, I wish we were practicing our tangent cycling and canoeing and hanging out up at our cabin." The Guy says.

"Oh yeah, that would be the life! We probably missed an upcoming race there was since we have been trapped here." Says the other Guy.

"You mean multiple?" Answers back, the other one and I hear them sigh. "We could have been running and swimming at the beach too while also doing a spot of fishing in our boat." Answers again the other, other Guy.

"Sounds like you both are real athletes, huh?" Cloud says, jumping in. The Guys nod excitedly, looking at each-other.

"Why won't you tell us you names?" Kelsey pipes up. They glare at her and shrug. Do they not know it?

"What would you be doing right now if you weren't here, Valerie?" The Guys ask me. Kelsey goes to answer for me, but then closes her mouth to let me if I want to answer for myself.

"Being normal..." I trail off. "Normal?" They ask perplexed. "Why?"

"Doesn't everyone want to fit in?" I respond.

"Well, I guess you're correct in that thinking." They respond together.

"Were students of magic from another world." Kelsey adds on.

"You weren't joking about that it seems..." They trail off.

"Anyway, be realistic. What would you want to be doing now?"

"Maybe reading...?" Is the one thing I say in response to such a question and they nod slowly. "Sounds like we all previously... Had it good maybe, but then again, so did many other members too." The Guys say.

"Yes. We did..." I hear an unfamiliar voice, but is female and we all, turning around to look at the door to see someone sliding in and gently closing the door behind her. "Avery!" Scream the two Guys, running up and hugging her. She gives them a quick hug back.

"You look tired." Louis comments. "Aren't we all?" She responds back, crossing her arms. Just then, I see she is wearing an armband and I rise to my feet slowly. "A-Avery.."

"Yes, Valerie?" She says, relaxing. "Y-Your arm!" I choke out. She looks sad. "Oh no." The two Guys say.

"You don't know how horrible it is to wake up and learn that your best friend, let alone the last living family member is gone. O-Owen gave me her team leader arm-band. Looks like I'm team leader now..." She says, sinking to her feet, wrapping her arms around her knees, rocking back and fourth.

I feel bad for her. This is horrible! She doesn't deserve to be going through this! "Valerie, before I ended up here with my family. We helped out to run a surf shack with our uncle.

I helped him out during the breaks when University wasn't running. I was studying for a degree in veterinary and to the side, I played guitar at the local bar all while having a love for the ocean. I swam and surfed and doing photography on the side. Taking photos and sometimes videos. The world I came from was lovely.

No doubt by now the Police have closed our missing person's case. All of ours infact, except for you and your friends.

You've been only here for a little while compared to us. Five years and now, Samantha is gone too."

"Avery..." Everyone chokes out, their eyes feeling with tears. She wipes the tears from her eyes. "I just want to sleep for a while." She says, laying down near the makeshift beds were the Guys having be staying and roll over to hug her on either side.

After this, we all settle down and go right back to bed too because we feel horrible and nothing else to do.

I'm rugged up and walking down to the cafeteria. I woke up feeling better, no doubt because of the medicine Owen gave me. I just wanted a little walk to clear my head. I see few members are out training in the snow or at the cafeteria, eating. I see Sam's flower is right where Ricky placed it.

No one around, I walk up to it, grabbing a seat to sit on and reach my finger out just to rest underneath it's petal's. "Hey Sam- Samantha." I say when I feel a strong grip slam up against some cupboards by my shoulders.

I open my eyes to meet Ricky's angry face. All the competitors are backing away in fright. "Don't you dare go near her, talk to her, breath on her or even look at her, squishy!" He yells at me, threateningly.

"It's bad enough that you are even in the same room as her. If I had my way, you'd be EATING YOUR FOOD OUT IN THE COLD FROM NOW ON FROM A DOG'S BOWL!"

I nod weakly, but then I hear a voice speak up. "As much as hate her too right now, *put* her down, Ricky."

That voice! I crane my neck to see who it is. It's Rain standing there with her hands on her hips and an annoyed expression. He lets go off me and I hit the floor hard, my rear end and tailbone hurting. Rain walks over, roughly pulling me to my feet and dusting me off, still looking quiet annoyed. "T-that-"

"Don't you even dare say it, Valerie! I DON'T want to even hear your voice, let along see you, but we can't everything we want in life can we? No! So I will settle for not hearing you speak!"

She lets go off me, walking over and pulling a tray of warm cupcakes out the oven and places them down on the island and pulling one out with some tongs and plonking it on a napkin and then reaches over to a 12 pack of water, grabbing one and shoves into my hands. "There, you have your food and water. Now go!" She snaps and I nod, hurrying away as fast as my legs can take me. Yikes!

After eating it and heading back to the dorms, I feel a strip of fabric tossed over my eyes and two sets of hands, covering my mouth and pulling me into a dark alleyway. I kick and squirm, but I'm just too weak.

I feel myself dragged for a little bit and I'm pushed into a chair, but whoever it is, does it very gently...

And my blind-fold is pulled off.

"Happy belated 18th birthday, Valerie!"

My jaw drops seeing my friends, Avery and the Guys from her team with paper party hats on their head. I look around seeing paper ring chains and papers lanterns, strung up, all over the room.

Even a couple balloons too.

"H-how?!" I choke out. "Owen surprisingly!" Kelsey smiles, giving me a hug and another kiss on my cheek. Louis looks a little shocked, then steps forward, placing a party hat on my head.

"This, 'observatory' looks great!" I cry. "We honestly didn't do much. Owen told us to 'vanish' and we came up here, finding all this. We don't have any presents for you, but we do have a cake! He said though, 'keep the noise down or the Guards on patrol will hear us so were going to be as quiet as possible, but still celebrate your birthday!" Cloud smiles.

I run around the room giving everyone a big hug and then we start to party as best we can. Owen had also left behind paper and other stationary for so we could make a paper pin the halo on the angel and other party games like that, we also have the blind-fold so we could put it on one of us then all spread out and the person it would have to wake around blind, trying to find someone.

I sat in front of my birthday cake.

"Happy birthday to you, happy birthday, dear, Valerie."

"Hip, hip!"

"Hooray!"

"Hip, hip!"

"Hooray!"

"Make a wish, Valerie." Avery smiles.

I wish to be able to go back home...

After this, Louis hands me the knife and I start cutting a piece for everyone.

Louis, Kelsey, Cloud, Avery, Guy #1, Guy #2 and lastly, Sam-Samantha. Everyone grabs their plate, sitting down to eat and then I realize I cut one too many...

She's not here to enjoy it... I sit looking at my piece and hers as the snow falls outside the window and the wind howling.

I sware I can almost see her in the sky outside the window. Hear her voice even.

She died for a cause. Our cause and I won't let her sacrifice or memory be in vain.

"Happy 18th birthday, Valerie."

"Thank you, Samantha."

Chapter 18

W e all meet up in the morning and head down to the cafeteria. When we arrive, we see everyone is already there and eating. "Food doesn't get served this early usually ..." I hear Louis comment.

"I wonder what certain people are planning..." I hear Cloud say with suspicion. Looking over I can see the Guards with Sebastian and Rain.

No, Owen...

"We all need to eat, we have no choice but to go there." I hear Avery speak up. "Yeah, you're right." Kelsey answers her and we all take a breath in, slowly walking in together.

I hear Ricky groan when he spots me. "Food's being served early today." Paige tells us, handing us some plates with food on it for us to take to our table.

We used to sit at different tables, but now we have just sort of taken to sitting together, both our teams after what we have been through. I take a sneaky look, seeing Sam's flower is still on the kitchen isle...

As we all sit, our jaws drop seeing that is proper food, but all fattening foods covered in sauces I physically can not stomach.

I look at Avery and the Guys to see them chowing away... The sight of it makes me want to be sick! I look over at my friends to see them eating too. I place my hands on my stomach, feeling the painful groan of hungriness, but I can't eat of any of this!

I push my plate away from me slowly and turn my head to look at Sebastian and Rain. A smirk is on their faces and then I lock eyes with Rain.

"Is something wrong, Valerie, dear?" I hear her taunt me. She knows all about my condition, what I can and can't eat.

I feel anger rising inside of me and I rise to my feet, I hear Avery drop her fork. "Valerie, what are you doing?!" I hear her whisper. "Valerie, what's upset you?" I hear Louis ask under his breath.

I push my chair back, turning around as quickly and angrily as possible. "Aww, seems like someone is a little angry today." I hear Rain tease, standing up with Sebastian.

"Something wrong, Sprout?" Sebastian says in a fake sweetness. "You knew, Rain! You knew!" I shout.

"Knew what?" She asks me back, looking confused. Great, she's playing dumb about it... I see Ricky's eyes are just waiting to burn into mine as he sits in the corner, observing me.

"Rain, I can't eat fatty food! I have anorexia!" I cry. I hear an audible gasp around the room. "Oh my god..." Cloud says.

She puts her hand on her chest. "Really? I would never have known, Valerie, dear. I am so, so, so sorry!" She says back in a sweet fake voice.

"Well, beggars can't be choosers unfortunately. We try to be accommodating. Maybe have a small taste?" I hear Sebastian comment back with his hands behind his back.

"No, you guys were aware of my illness from day one! There's always something easy to digest here."

"Aw, well, let's just say that perhaps I'm angry with a certain so and so who went out into the frozen wastelands and that I had to waste my time looking for her to save her sorry ass. Wouldn't you agree, Sprout?"

I grit my teeth and clench my fists. "I cannot believe any of you! Do you even realize that Sam was the leader and not me?! I'm not pinning this on her, but we all agreed that every one of us would go out there, together rather than stay here with the likes of you all!"

I see Ricky stand up angry. "Go ahead and push my buttons, Valerie. It will not end well for you if I get to have my way!" He yells.

I decide I've had enough and give him a rather rude gesture with my finger. I hear him stomp his foot and let out a raged yell.

"Alright, alright, enough! You have made your statement, Sprout. You can leave here while your friends all enjoy this delicious breakfast. Now go, but may I sincerely remind you that, you are the one who *begged* me to bring you home from the Frozen Wasteland." Sebastian chuckles and I feel Rain grab my upper forearm, pulling me away from the cafeteria and my friends.

It hurts hearing my friends call my name, but soon it fades as Rain roughly forces me to walk with her.

"Where are you taking me?!" I cry trying to pull away, but she only grips on tighter and says nothing. "Rain!" I yell and she stops.

"What, Valerie?!" She snaps. "Where. Are. You. Taking. Me?!" I yell back.

"Getting you out of Sebastian's way for the moment." She retorts back.

"And you're dragging me back to the sleeping quarters?!"

"That's the plan, Valerie, dear" She responds gripping my arm tighter and pulling me towards the sleeping quarters.

When we arrive, she unlocks our door and pulls me inside. "Stay here." She says, mildly annoyed, pushing me and I hit the floor. "Wait, please don't do this! I beg of you! Rain, please!"

I cry, trying to stand up in time, but all I manage is to grab the door handle after she has closed the door and I hear the door lock.

Banging my wrists on the door, I yell for her to come back and let me out but all I hear is her distant laugh and the words that I take some time to, 'cool off.' I sink down, back against the door and pull my knees up, under my chin and wrap my arms around them, feeling tears start to slide down my cheeks.

I stay there, my back against that door for what feels like literally hours. I do stand up every so often and head to the bathroom to drink from the tap so I don't end up dehydrating, but other than that I am beyond hungry. I also step out onto the balcony, but there is no way off it from here and I can see everyone has vanished from the cafeteria.

No members, my friends, leaders or Guards. This makes me feel really uncomfortable...

I lean back against the door again, sitting there for countless more hours till I see the day become afternoon...

I feel the wooden door hit my back, knocking me flat on to my stomach.

When did I fall asleep?!

"Get up, Valerie Woods."

It's Rain. I sit up slowly, rubbing my sore eyes and muscles. I see her standing there, but there is someone else behind her which I can't quite make out.

I hear something drop onto the floor.

I look over seeing something, but it is in a packet...

"Hurry up and eat it. Sebastian wants you." She scolds me roughly and pulling me up off the floor to drag me some- where. I grab the food just in the nick of time as we leave.

She keeps a tight grip on me again, but she leads me over to their house as I slurp. It's yogurt and doesn't really fill me up.

Soon we arrive at a big room with a mahogany desk, chan- delier on the roof and large windows. Rain lets go out of me, I race over the windows, putting my hands on it to look out.

"You can see the whole city from here!" I exclaim and noticing people walking around now. I can see my Friends down below running towards the sleeping quarters. No! They aren't going to find me there because I'm here where they can't see me!

"That glass is sound & shatterproof, you know?" I hear Rain say from behind me. She's got her arms folded and blocking my only exit, aka our point of entry.

"Why don't you go take a seat while we wait for my hubby, hm?" I hear Her suggest and I growl, walking over to the fancy desk and sit right on-top which annoys her slightly.

"You didn't say where." I laugh. "Okay, fine. You can have that 1 point, geez." She mumbles back. Slight victory! At-least I took her down a notch slightly.

After what feels like forever, I hear the sound of footsteps and I look up, seeing Rain move aside. It's Sebastian and he claps his hands together, approaching me. "Ah, Valerie, you came."

"It's not like I had much of a choice!" I growl. "Aw, well. A slight oversight, Valerie Does it really matter?" He says, pushing up the glasses on his nose a bit with his finger.

I go to speak, but he shushes me and takes a seat at the desk in which I jump off, retreating, but Rain shoves me forwards away from the exit that I end up standing before Sebastian.

"Do you know why I have summoned you here?" He asks me. I shake my head.

He stands up, walking over the window and signals for me to follow him. "When you look out there, Sprout. What stands out to you?" He asks me.

Why is he being cryptic? "Bravery, selflessness. My friends." I retort.

"Huh, really. I see a foolish girl who thinks she is better than us, knows better than me. Having friends will only drag you down.

You saw where it got poor Samantha. She's dead because of you, Valerie. You're still alive so that is something you still have compared to her.

She lost everything including her life."

"None of that is on me, Sebastian. She made her decision and so did I. We all did." I say back, but he doesn't even flinch.

"You know something, Sprout. Regardless, I would have never left you out there to die in that snow. You're too valuable to me. Can't have you dying on me, now can we?"

"But Sam is dead. Isn't she worth just as much as my life?"

"No, not really. She's human and before we accelerated you and your friends, we tested your abilities.

You're a diamond in the rough. You're stronger than your friends. Why do you hide it?"

"What are you saying?! You tried to save Emily's life, didn't you?"

"Nah. One you've seen one Human, you've seen em all. Saving her would not be worth it."

"So you are saying that you let her die from Merge poisoning and did nothing to help her?!"

I hear him clap. "You guessed correctly. You really are a smart one, Valerie.

You'll go far, but, you're not at the level I wished you were. If you didn't keep angering me, getting sick, you would have attended training. Frankly, I think were both gonna have a little problem now. Don't you agree?"

I gulp, not knowing what to say to this. He turns around to face me. "Do you know what it means to be elite?"

I shake my head. "No idea."

"It means being the best." He says a second after. I see him him a button on his desk and a room opens off to to the side.

It's adorned with hundreds of clothes on racks, shoes on display on their boxes.

"This is our hall of elites. Step closer and have a look." He says, pushing me forward by his hand on my back that I have no choice, but to head deep into the room. I eye the suspicious coat and scarf from Owen's observatory hanging up and Rain directs me to some clothing on a mannequin in the middle.

It reminds me of the armor, uniform people like Ryland wore before our city was reformed, but this is sturdier, brighter.

"What did you think of it, Valerie?" I hear him question. "It's beautiful. Looks expensive and really high quality..." I respond, seeing Rain looking at a green coat and ruby rimmed glasses the same shelf as the coat and scarf that belongs to Owen.

"You know something, Valerie? You remind me of a girl named Dana in your personality and spirit. You're both the same in every way, but. Well, let me tell you something. You both have one thing that sets you apart from each-other.

She was obedient in the end, and you? You are not. You have been a pain in my butt since day 1 that you ended up here."

"Then let me and my friends go home! That way we will be out of your hair."

"And why would I do a thing like that?"

"Because it's the right thing to do and you should let everyone else here go home too." I respond and I see him shake his head.

"Not happening. You're a diamond in the rough. I just told you that, Valerie. I would like to see you from now on co-operate with me, with us. Would that be so hard?"

I feel my anger boiling. "I'll never co-operate with you, Sebastian!" I yell and I spit at him too which cuts him off guard. Rain looks shocked too.

"Really?"

"Yes."

"Fine, be like that, Valerie. But remember. I control your destiny and if there is something that I want you to do then I will do it and you will do it too."

"What is that supposed to mean?" I ask and I feel him grab me my my clothing, throwing me into the wall next to the armor.

"Sebastian, stop this, please! Why me?! Why am I so special compared to others? I don't understand it! I'm not special!"

"You're telling me that you haven't figured it out, Sprout? You're the one person who has ever really stood up to me without backing down even a little to avoid a fight and I have a problem with that also.

You know, here's what I suggest. I will give you a second chance to play my games and do as I ask or well, I can't promise no harm will come to you or your friends from now on in the future. Your answer, Valerie?"

I look at him in shock. His going to do something to us and me if I don't start doing what he wants from now on...

"Tick, tock, the clock is running away from us, Valerie" I hear him say. I sigh and open my mouth to give my answer.

"Yes, okay, fine! Whatever you want!"

"Good. I'm glad that you have come around, Valerie. We both shall start seeing eye to eye from now on, hmm?"

I feel him grip my arm, pulling me to my feet. "You know something also, Valerie?"

"What?"

"I want to see how the armor looks on you. Put it on." And he let's go off my arm. Seriously? He wants me to just put the armor on in-front of him and his wife?

I just stand there, not moving. "I don't see you doing as I'm asking, Valerie." I hear him say.

A few seconds pass and I see him getting angrier. "Ricky!" He yells and I see him walk in. "What, boss?" He asks.

"Go catch our little friend, Avery for me, will you? Take her down to my lab and restrain her. I'll be down there soon." Sebastian says to which Ricky leaves.

I put my hands up. "Wait, wait! I'll do it! Okay?! I'm doing it!" I say.

"Go on, show me and my wide here then." He retorts. I put the armor on over my clothes so they can see.

I hear Sebastian clap his hands. "What do you think, darling?" He says addressing her and places his hand on her shoulders as she walks right up to him.

"Splendidly obedient, but also elite." She answers.

"Yes." I hear him respond back. "Take the armor off. You can go back now, Dana. Uh- I mean Valerie." He taunts.

I take the armor off as they both laugh at me and they let me leave their office.

Chapter 19

I am just full on seething! I feel like my heart and my head are just boiling now and that I have just been pushed to my limit, pretty much. "Move out of my way, shortie."

I feel someone shove me and I look up seeing it was Ricky, walking through. I turn my head seeing my friends, the Guys from Avery's team and the other community members are here eating. They haven't noticed me yet. I honestly feel like I can't take it anymore that I sink to the ground, kneeling over and clutching my hair with my fingers to the point that I'm going to pull strands of hair out, hurting myself.

I see Avery isn't here. "Hey, what are you doing?" I hear Paige ask, noticing me. She places her hand on his shoulder to get his attention. "Are you okay, Valerie?" She asks a second later, showing a slight hint of genuine kindness.

"Valerie?" I hear Kelsey whimper, standing up, having noticed me. The rest of our team does and so does the Guys. "Hey! You seen, Avery?" One of them asks. I grit my teeth and pull at my shirt feeling like it's constricting me. "Valerie?" I hear Ricky address me, actually bending down to my level.

"Are you actually okay? Do you want us to call Owen down here?" He asks weirdly, showing genuine concern. His eyebrows are raised including his eyes. I say nothing, just sort of glaring then, anger burning in my eyes. "Okayyy, I don't think she's okay. Call Owen down here." Ricky says back to Paige and I see her walk over to pick up a walkie talkie.

And then it's just like a part of me snaps. I stand up, moving awkwardly that I'm hardly standing straight. "She's dead, Ricky. Because of me, but also Sebastian. They could have saved her, but they didn't. They let Merge poison her and they saved me instead of her because apparently I'm a 'diamond in the rough!'"

"I-I-I... what are you talking about, Valerie? I d-don't und erstand..." Ricky stammers looking really confused and distressed by what I'm saying. "WHY ARE THEY DOING THIS TO ME?!" I yell with tears brimming my eyes. "Hey, hey. Stop! Stop, please!" He begs me, approaching me to place his hand on my shoulders to calm me. I see him pull out a handkerchief from his pocket. "Y-you're going to cause yourself a panic attack. I don't want to see you get to that point, Valerie... It's a horrible experience..."

"NO!" I scream, fighting to get his hands off me. "Call Owen, anytime now!" I hear Ricky freak out. "Owen, are you there?" I hear Paige cry into her walkie talkie. "GET OFF ME!" I yell.

I somehow find the strength to push him aside to the floor. My friends and the other members are literally horrified, watching this scene unfold. I stagger forward, gripping the Island with one of my hands and my head with my other hand. V-Valerie..." I hear Ricky say, sitting up slowly and carefully. A bruise forming on the side of his head. He must have hit the bench on the way down.

I feel my arm just swipe and it collides with something thin and glass, breaking that shards pierce my skin, embedding while the rest goes all over the bench and I watch slowly as a white flower gently sails in the end, stained with my blood on the ends of it fairly heavily.

And then the official sound of glass breaking happens and I step back, my head's throbbing violently, not even registering the pain in my arm. I turn my head seeing a horrified look on Ricky and Paige's face. Tears are in his eyes and Paige has dropped the walkie talkie, pieces of it broken, lying on the floor.

Ricky stands up slowly, taller than me, a look of disbelief on his face, his expression changing to one of anger. I hear Kelsey cry and trying to reach me, but the Guys from Avery's team are holding her back. He raises his hand and I turn my head, eyes closed, prepared to accept what his about to do to me...

I wait for it, but it doesn't come. Slowly opening my eyes, I see him slowly lower his hand, turning to Paige. "Don't just stand there, useless... Get a dust pan and brush." He says to her and then he turns back to look at me, a look of pain in his eyes, even slight tears forming.

"Is what you said about Sam, you and Sebastian true?" He chokes out and I give a small nod.

Then I see a shadow on the snow covered ground in front of me and before I can turn my head, I feel a sharp prick in my shoulder, but they take it out gently afterwards and I feel myself hit the cold ground. "You should take her to your room to sleep it off and calm down. I don't know what Rain or Sebastian said to upset her, but..."

It's Owen's voice and I pass out completely.

"Y-yes, Owen."

"Thank you, Louis."

It's been hours since I accidentally broke Sam's flower... I-I don't know if Ricky is angry or more upset at me. It wasn't intentional, but I'm thankful that he didn't hit me. He could have, but he chose not too. Unfortunately, what happened didn't calm me down anymore or make anything better. Owen showed up to help me. Yeah, he sticked a needle in my shoulder which knocked me out for a few hours, but it didn't solve anything or my feelings!

I woke up in the in my bed in my room, my Friends also by my side. They told me what happened, but told me to rest. I haven't seen the Guys from Avery's team. No doubt they are shaken by what I said and that... Avery is now missing. I have no doubt this has Sebastian all over it... He was going to use her as a bargaining chip against me, but I hope she's okay!

Why hasn't she come back though? It worries me... I take a deep breath in, feeling the cold chilly air as I sit outside on a plastic chair of our balcony. My friends are all inside asleep except for me. It's super late at night! I just needed some fresh air and here I am.

I can't help feeling like I'm 100% responsible for everything that has happened here. If it weren't for me... We wouldn't have ended up here or stuck in this world. I'm weak and my friends have been selflessly taking care of me. I should be the one taking care of them and supporting them, listening to them! But instead it's been all about me! I'm the most selfish person in the world right now!

I risked their lives including four more, one of which lost hers because of me... This all my fault! I silently cry into my hands, kneeling over, praying that my Friends won't wake up and hear me.

Oh, I so hope that they don't. I head back inside to grab a quick cup of water and take it back out with me to drink on the veranda, the cup is shaking so bad in my shaky hands, some water tips over the edges of the cup onto the pavement. I drink the water, then place the cup down. I'm still shaking heavily and step forward to the railing, resting my hands on it as I take a shaky breath, the cold leaving my mouth in a small cloud. You can't see the aurora from here, just mountains and trees, the odd polar bear, but it's still really beautiful!

Shame though that such a nice world is the home to two not so *nice* people. I honestly feel so guilty right now for just everything that is happening. It's to the point I can't handle it anymore and before I know it... I'm doing something reckless.

I'm sitting on the edge of the balcony, my legs over just dangling above the hard snow covered ground, I'm shaking and my fingers are turning red from gripping the rail so strongly at that I'm just here in the cold, outside at Night. I glance at the analog clock and the hands seem to be stuck trying to tick from 12.

I take a shaky breath inching myself forward more and more when I notice down below a Guard. Ricky in particular. His rugged up warm and his eyes are wide. His seen me and what I'm about to do... He yells something out that I can't quite make out to his partner, Paige and she books it for the leaders home.

I hear the sound of a door opening and some random member has stepped onto the balcony of her team's room. She looks shocked and I hear her whisper something back, walking back into her dorm. "Hey Guys, one of the other other members, those ones who upset Sebastian alot is on the edge of her railing.... Yeah, their team leader! She's totally goanna commit-"

"Valerie, what are you doing?!"

I flinch, hearing my name called and look back to see Kelsey awake and standing on the balcony behind me. Snow flurries are getting caught in blonde hair that's out of it's scrunchies, gently blowing in the wind much like mine. "Just go back inside, Kelsey..." I mumble.

She takes a step forward. "No, you're my friend and you're goanna-"

I shuffle a-bit forward. "Woah, hey, hey, no! I'll step back okay if it means you don't shuffle forward, Valerie.."

"Kelsey, just please go back inside!"

"I can't do that, Valerie. Look where you are right now. I've been in your position before you know? We ignored your eating disorder because we didn't know how to talk about and to help you. I haven't suffered from anorexia, but I do have bulimia, you know? Four years ago, Louis saved my life. I'm just like you! If you go through with this you-you will... and if not, you could be heavily paralyzed!"

"Kelsey, stop! Please. Don't you understand why I'm doing this?"

"No, I don't, Valerie, but y-you can tell me! Just let me help you back onto the veranda and we can sit down together, inside. I can listen, Valerie."

"No."

"Okay... w-we don't need to go inside, but I still want to be there for you and listen. I'm your Friend and you have always been there for me in my opinion. It's time I payed back the favor. Tell me what you're thinking, Valerie, please."

"Right now?"

"Yes..."

I sigh and go over to her, climbing off the edge of the balcony. I see her relax a little bit. "I don't feel like I can take it anymore. The temperatures, the way were treated by the Guards and how the other other members gossip behind our backs, the lack of food and water, healthcare. I thought we were free and all it did was cost us... A friend and then were back here and they are angrier than ever, Kelsey. They humiliated me earlier and they are just goanna keep making it worse for me and...

I'm in love with Louis. He likes you."

"What? Valerie, he likes you too-"

"But not in the same way."

She holds up her hand. "I understand, Valerie. This is hard and having emotions makes it worse.

We can talk about this further inside and I want you to know that I really like you too. I'm... Polyamorous. I haven't told anyone. Maybe, if you want... You and I and Louis can all be together? I've denied it for the longest time, but I'm actually attracted to both of you.

I don't know how Louis would feel about it. Do you think I'm disgusting now that I've told you? Crap, I shouldn't have said anything."

Seems this has been chewing up on the inside for ages...

"Sorry, I'm making it worse, I'm being selfish by talking about me-"

"No, it's okay." I tell her.

"Uh, anyway... You're than welcome to come share my bed with me, my blankets are really fluffy, we can wrap ourselves under them. Better than staying out here in the cold..."

I think about it. "I don't want you to give up, Valerie. You have alot to live for. We can walk this road together can't we, yeah? I regularly attend therapy. I can help you with the process in the future when we get back home so you're not afraid. It's no wonder that you were desperate to escape from what seemed like being locked up in your mind." She says, stepping closer to me. I panic and quickly step back onto the balcony, but she's quicker than me and actually stronger. She wraps her arms around my waist and pulls me of. I don't want to hurt her in a struggle so I let go. She hugs me on the floor, head resting on my shoulder and I feel her cold lips plant a gentle kiss on my neck.

"Please don't blame yourself, this isn't your fault. None of why were here and what happened here is your fault." She tells me with tears in her eyes. I go to speak, but she shushes me just stroking my back and hair too. I let out a sigh. "Just, please don't scare me like that ever again you idiot!" She chastises. "And we can both love, Louis, you hear? We'll work this out, I'm not out to be your rival over us liking the same guy, Valerie."

I nod in her arms. "It's cold out here, Kelsey." I whimper, feeling tears fall.

"Yeah, it is. Let's go back inside to bed where it's warm, Valerie. Just please... Promise me that you won't blame yourself going forward okay? You usually blame things that go wrong on yourself... I've seen happen in class. And don't try to hurt yourself either.. We can be here for you. All of us, your friends. We'll learn about your condition and how to support your, what you think us doing for you would be helpful." She responds back.

"Only if you promise not to blame yourselves either for this situation." I choke out. "All of you, every one of you."

"Fair call!" She says, stifling a laugh. She helps me to my feet, but not letting go of me as she guides me back inside, closing the door behind us to keep the snow out. I feel her give the top of my head a kiss.

We step back into the room and I gulp see Louis and Cloud are awake and out of bed, their arms crossed.

"G-Guys, I-I-"

"You don't need to say anything, Valerie. We saw and heard every word. This is going to be alot of processing and talking now." Louis says, arms folded, but his not cross, more concerned.

"You both could really hurt yourselves!" Cloud yells at me and Kelsey to which I sadly nod, still in her arms.

"Valerie, come here." Louis and Cloud say together, them wrapping their arms around me and Kelsey as we all sink to our bedroom together. "Thank you." I choke out. "No problem, were here for you. Both of you." Louis answers. "And were not leaving, nor giving up." Kelsey and Cloud say together.

A knock is heard against our door. We all stand up, Kelsey still hugging me as the others have let go, but Louis is standing beside us and Cloud goes to slowly open it and see who it is for us.

We see him shoved aside, hitting the floor. He sits up fairly quickly, but is heavily disoriented. I see Louis backing away. Why?

"Where is she?! Is she okay?!"

It's Ricky. "I-I'm right here, R-Ricky!" I choke out. "Oh, thank the gods if they're watching!" I hear Ricky say. I look past him seeing other Guards dealing with the other gawking members.

"And then three sets of individuals step into the room that I wish didn't. Sebastian, Rain and Owen who are in their p.j's.

"She's okay!" Ricky cries out, but I just see Sebastian cross his arms. Rain is too, but Owen actually looks genuinely concerned. "Do you think you could all leave?!" I hear Cloud snap.

"Oh, I don't think so. No." Sebastian says back to Cloud. I and Kelsey start to step back slowly from them. Just... They don't let us, I gasp feeling Sebastian and Rain grab onto either side of me. I squirm. Ricky pushes Kelsey away, knocking her to the floor. She let's out a squeal and Louis has to help her up. "Let me go!" I cry. "Nope, I'm afraid we can't do that, Sprout." Sebastian answers.

My friends look absolutely traumatized. I feel Sebastian and Rain start to pull me from the room despite my kicking and screaming which does no good.

"Where are you taking her?!" I hear Kelsey cry. "No, bring her back!" I hear Kelsey cry in absolute hysterics.

"Kelsey... Sebastian, Rain and I are going to take Valerie somewhere safe for a bit. This is for her own safety." I hear Owen tell them as he stays back to talk to them.

I cry out for my friends, but it does no good. "What are you g-going to do to me?!" I cry.

"You'll find out soon enough, Sprout." I hear Sebastian comment. "Please!" I cry, but it does no good and soon enough we have stepped into their home and I feel myself black out.

Chapter 20

The room I'm in is small and the lights are off, door closed is fine with me. I listen gently in the atmosphere, not a sound is able to be heard except for the gentle spinning of a fan above me that is slowly turning and the hum of a heater that is also in the room, but like it's on standby.

All that is in this room other than the bed I'm on which I notice is portable meaning it can be transported from one place to another is one beside table each with a small lamp on it and a wooden, but also fabric based chair that looks comfy, but light weight to move around.

This room doesn't have any windows though that I can look out to see the night sky or the sun of and there is a small viewing window in the door.

I relax, feeling really calm unsure if it's me not stressing out or the medicine I've probably been drugged with. I thought Sebastian and Rain were going to do worse to me... Horrible things. This environment is more homely and less clinical than all the other rooms I've in before when I've awoken from being passed out somehow...

This peace I'm feeling right now is nice and I feel myself drifting back into a gentle, calming sleep of my own free will.

I'm waking up again, but this time it's because there is a slight disturbance in the room. I can hear what sounds like paper shuffling and the gentle scribble of a pen. I realize that my sleeve has been pulled up a bit on my right arm and something is wrapped around it, gently squeezing it, but not constricting it. What could it be? Why?

Well, at-least I know I can form conscious thoughts without problem! That's good, really good.

"Evening, Valerie."

I let out a slight whimper upon hearing a voice. It's male, but sounds gentle and the accent is a little cultural... Not like Sebastian's at all. At least I know it's not him which is a relief. Opening my eyes and gently turning my head, it's Owen. "Sorry about the noise and my unexpected intrusion while you were sleeping the sedative off. I was just coming in here to check your blood pressure, pulse, any signs of fever, your breathing. Things like that, y-you know as I'm a doctor...

We didn't know if you had swallowed anything o-or yeah beforehand. I also wanted to check up on you periodically as I didn't know how your body would react to the sedative. You can never be too careful, I say."

"S-Sedative?!"

"Yes... You don't remember?"

"No..."

I watch as Owen takes a seat near me and he undoes the blood pressure cuff around my arm, placing it on his lap and gently rolling my sleeve down. He takes my hand in his palm, gently turning it over and stretching out my fingers lightly and massaging my wrist.

"That feels nice..." I trail off, only earning a small, "Mmm." from him.

"Valerie, you were onto the edge of your team's dormitory's balcony. Ricky came to our home, waking us all saying that you looked like you were going to jump. After we arrived, you seemed fine, but also highly agitated and... Rain alongside Sebastian helped to bring you to a place of safety. The hospital is kind of over compacity so we brought you to our house, it's quite large.

The medicine you were on wore off and you became agitated again so I administered a light sedative again. It's the next day in the evening.

I've been checking on you about every 20 minutes. It's about 4 a.m right now and you seem like you are doing better. You were crying so much and screaming before that you were becoming dehydrated. I felt administering was the best choice to prevent you from falling further and to save you from any potential emotional harm or injury that you could have caused yourself if we let it... Go on."

"W-where are my f-friends?" I choke out in response to everything he just told me.

"I stayed behind to speak with them and explain the situation.

I'm going to just look after you a little while here. What you did was scary and could have turned into a very serious situation... Your team right now are back in bed asleep. Kelsey Launceston was it?"

"Yes, sir."

"You don't need to be so formal with me, Owen will do. Anyway, Kelsey, she was quiet upset as well. I felt bad, but I feel you deserve to know. I gave her a light sedative as well and right now, she's sleeping it off much like you were, but surrounded by the rest of your friends, safe back in the dormitory.

She was very worried about you. Anyway, I think you both are going to recover fine. I will drop by before breakfast and check up on her, but right now, I'm here to support you."

I nod, just listening to his soothing voice while also taking in everything his telling me. "Why are you doing this, Owen?" I whisper.

He turns bright red in the face. "Uh, uh, uh, I'm not saying you're a replacement, but you uh..."

"I what?" I snap, sitting up. "Woah, hey, no, lie down! I don't want you to sit up, not after what you've been through! Just lie back down, it's okay." He panics, forcing me to lie down.

"What is it you're trying to say? Spit it out!" I cry.

He sighs.

"Okay, I want you to know that despite my bad choice of friends, believe I'm aware... I believe that I do try to be a good person and a good doctor. I care about anyone who comes in my door, but... You've heard about Dana who used to live here in this community I'm sure.

She suffered Anorexia too and despite our best efforts to help her get better, they weren't enough. We failed and if I ever get a 2nd chance to make things right for her, I will. But alas, she was one of the victims who count towards the high mortality rate your illness holds, Valerie.

We- Well, more I didn't want to see another life lost to it and... You remind me of Dana as well. Not just because her and you both starved yourselves or alternated between eating and restricting, but I like you...

You're pretty, you're brave, considerate, friendly, fair, loyal, a good tutor and role-model, I'd say even a leader. All things Dana and one of her friends was... It doesn't come along often. It's what Sebastian and Rain call: 'Elite', but I say it's just something that makes one human.

People are inherently good or bad, but people tend to err on one side more than the other and the qualities in you are the same qualities that we saw in Dana and a friend of hers. The perfect role-model leader, but also sassy, easily emotional and more. You all did well at balancing out who you guys were despite the problems you all had.

All people have problems. Anyway, enough about them... They're dead, we can't change the past and you seem to be doing so much better than earlier now, Valerie when we first brought you in here. You're not a Dana replacement in my eyes, okay?"

I nod, not seething, but uncomfortable and I don't know what to say so I opt for ignoring this talk of Dana.

"Was Kelsey able to breathe? Was her chest hurting, was she in pain?! She can sometimes can have panic attacks and- and-"

But he doesn't let me finish, placing my hand down gently and cupping my knee. "Kelsey is going to be just fine. As you will be too." He says, trying to soothe me once again.

I look away from Owen for a bit, just staring up at the, slowly rotating fan. I feel him pat my knee, then remove his hand and standing up. "You're tired, I'll let you rest a bit more. Then come see you again about 5:30 a.m, okay? I have some Hospital rounds to do."

"N-no, wait!" I choke out.

"Yes...?" He says slowly, an eyebrow raising.

"S-Sam-"

"Samantha, our former security guard?"

"Yes!"

"What about her, Valerie? You're tired and do need your sleep. We can talk more later in the morning. You don't need to deprive yourself of sleep."

"W-why did you let her die? You could have saved her and you didn't. Sebastian should not have been allowed to perform her surgery! H-He didn't even try to save her from exposure to Merge, Owen!"

I see Owen's eyes go wide at the words I just spoke. I see him take a seat again, bending down to me and he places his palm on my forehead.

"It's warm. You have a slight fever. It's not too bad, I can get you a cold cloth."

"Owen, Sam!"

"I heard what you said, Valerie."

"Then why are you taking my temperature?!"

"Samantha's not dead, Valerie. Why do you think that? Where did you hear that? Or is it a conclusion that you came to draw in your own mind?"

I stare up at him like that his a total idiot. What the flip is he talking about?! I'll play along for now... "B-but if she's n-not d-dead like we w-were told then where i-is she?!

Why hasn't she came back to the city? Avery's the leader of her friends small knit group now!"

"It's sad to say this Valerie, but she's currently unfit right now to be out and about, leading her team to potential victory in Rain and Sebastian's sick, twisted ideas of fun. She's alive, but in a coma. Merge is deadly. I'm glad Sebastian was able to make an antidote from Merge for her, but if she will wake up now or not is a waiting game, really."

"I'm so confused, Owen!" I tell him and then it hits me. Did I transition between outcomes while I was asleep? Shit, it's bad if I have!

"Valerie, what were you seeing, hearing or even thinking the last few days then?" He responds, standing up.

"I'm going to get you some medicine for your fever and in the mean time, I'm going to speak with Sebastian and Rain. We didn't know how sick you were, especially after going out into the frozen wasteland by yourself."

"By. My. Self?!"

"Yes. Sam followed you out there to bring you back after your friends reported you missing..."

"Then what is or isn't my reality anymore?!" I cry, upset even though I know he won't understand me. "Where do I belong, Owen?!"

"That's not something I can help you with overnight, Valerie. We need to get you more well now and then we join up our 'timelines' so to speak of what happened to you while you were slightly off the deep end. I don't believe you're psychotic per say, okay?

Look, I think you should sleep now, Valerie for a bit. I need to go and speak with Rain, Sebastian and the Guards. I'm sorry."

He says tucking me in and leaving the room. I hear the door lock after his left. A headache is pounding against the inside of my skull making it hard to sleep, but somehow I do fall back to sleep and drift off into it deeply.

Chapter 21

Have I really been out of it like Owen told me? Because even if is this another outcome of this timeline, I'm still me and if I've behaving the way he said I was, it means... I am truly unstable.

I can't begin to imagine what it was like for my friends that I love, seeing me in such a state if what I was told was true and where do I go from here?

Knocking on my door occurs. I shake my head to clear my thoughts after hearing a series of short knocks on the door. "W-who-" but I don't get to finish asking as the door slides open gently and someone is poking their head in.

"R-Ricky..." I choke out seeing it's him. He nods, looking down with a sad expression. His not wearing his on duty, guard uniform.

"G-Good m-morning, Valerie Woods..."

His stumbling over his words, his nervous standing infront of me! I squeeze my eyes shut. "Hey, hey, I-I don't want you to b-be scared of me right now. I k-know how vulnerable you are right now and all, but-but Owen wanted me to bring you some breakfast."

I open my eyes seeing him holding a plate of simple, only buttered toast and a cup of hospital grade orange juice. "D-do you want it, Valerie? You don't have to take it, but you just haven't been eating much and I-I will admit it that perhaps I was taking my invisible anger out on you, depriving y-you of food. I just-just wanted to tell you that I'm sorry.

I w-worry that this is my fault and I was the one w-who might have p-pushed you t-to blindly walk off into the snow and-and for you to try-try... Well, it doesn't matter now I guess.

T-the d-damage has already been done now, I suppose..." He says placing the plate on the beside table and his kneeling over, shaking and clutching his elbows in his hands.

I ignore the food, not feeling hungry. "I-I'm so c-c-c-c-"

"Cold? Oh, no, wait, confused!" He asks, finishing my sentence. I nod. He looks to the door and gently closes it and takes a seat near my bed.

"We won't have long. Ask me any question you want, Valerie. I'll tell you the truth. I p-promise!"

"I don't know what is real or not real anymore, Ricky."

"I know, neither do I or my friends somedays and I don't even know how to make it up to you at this point, Valerie..."

"Is Sam alive?"

He nods slowly, looking to his feet, hands shaking in his lap. "Y-your t-team reported you m-missing and we spotted you walking off into the snow. You had somehow snuck out.

Samantha went after you to bring you b-back. I-I loved h-her even though she was no longer a Guard, we grew quite close during the time she was and I reported to the leaders that you... Yeah, it took days, but we finally found you... It was at the cost of Samantha though...

I have never seen someone as small as you survive in a frozen wasteland on their own. I and my friends are literally asking each-other how you survived days out there, no food or water including the distance you walked and crossing a frozen river including climbing a mountain cliff face.

W-when we f-found you lying in the snow, you were h-hardly breathing...

Samantha did catch up to you at one point, but you fought with her and the river, frozen over, cracked. She fell into the water which is tainted from Merge and you ran.

Were all relieved that you hadn't been exposed to Merge, but you were highly feverish. Maybe you just s-snapped because of me and how... they-they... nevermind... Treated you and your brain just went on flight mode, auto-pilot or something. We don't really understand what happened to you and then you t-tired to... yeah..."

I close my eyes shaking, taking in every word. "W-what about the white f-flower and yelling at me?"

He rubs his neck. "Flower? S-sorry, I don't understand. Anyway, I was treating you horribly at one point. I-I was angry at the fact Samantha went after you, but you were out there alone.

Without her... It might have been too late to save you so maybe she did the right thing despite the fact how much she- I- we hated you or what we thought of you. She let you run when we she did catch up to you also. Anyway, I was angry and upset and have been taking my anger out on you, further worsening your psychotic state.

I don't know what was going on inside your head, but I clearly made it worse. I was angry, but I'm glad your alive. I blamed Sam's comatose state on you... I made an example of you, yelled at you infront of everyone. It's too early to know if she will wake up yet... Merge is deadly..."

"Are you telling me that Sam suffered alone?!" I choke out.

He nods slowly. "She was struggling to breathe when we found her. What followed was so much worse... A part of me wished you had stayed with her, but your mind was elsewhere and you didn't know what you were doing or what was happening."

I clutch my hair between my fingers, crying. "Hey, hey, let go, let go1 I-I don't want you to hurt yourself! Maybe I s-shouldn't have t-told you any of this... You might not have been ready. Owen won't be happy with me."

"He won't find out if I don't tell him, Ricky" I respond. "Thank you." He says, wiping a tear.

"I'm glad you were honest with me..." I tell him.

"Anyway, look, I can't hang around here much longer. I have to go on duty, I'm sorry." He says, standing up and heading to the door. "We've been taking advantage of your already vulnerable state from the start, Valerie when you and your friends ended up here. What happens here on out might not be pleasant for you, Valerie, but I want you to know I'm on your side, okay? If you really need anything or any help, just talk to me if we see eachother... But I'm not looking to lose my job though."

And then he leaves pretty much, I leap out of bed, grabbing his arm before he can close the door and I look up to him with pleading eyes that he can't ignore.

"Please don't leave me. I need help, I need answers!"

He kneels down, placing his hands on the sides of my shoulders. "You are one heck of a person, Valerie! A real survivor. You know that? Five minutes and then I will bring you back and you finish sleeping, eat your breakfast too." He says gently taking my hand as we creep through the corridor.

I and Ricky are down low, listening into Sebastian, Rain & Owen talking. I gulp, seeing Shelby in the corner of the room playing with Declan...

I knew it was too good to be true! No wonder Sebastian didn't believe me as she isn't missing in this outcome! He thought I had lost it which I have now apparently... This makes me feel sad for her that she's here living a life that's... Wait... how do I even know that her life is unbearable... goddammit. I don't- I don't know anything about her!

What of it's not?! Wait... Where's Harriet? Does she escape in both outcomes?

"Where's Harriet?" I whisper slowly to Ricky. "Girl ran away, don't know why. One of the members from the other side of town where people are banished too for non-compliance, but not bad enough to be jailed have vanished too..." He says turning back to spy on the leaders with me. I clutch my head, shaking it and I feel his hand grip my shoulder, squeezing it a bit to help ground me back in reality.

"I really think we should send Valerie and her friends home. This isn't even their world, they're not supposed to be in this timeline! And her health at this point in my opinion is at risk. Medical and psychological. Valerie is clearly not well enough or cut out for this community much like Dana and even Scout wasn't. When they all first arrived here, it was clear she was sick from weeks trapped in the hallway of star-gates, Including her friends.

Let's just send them home and they can get her some healthcare. Right now, we have her under observation and do you know who is going to be the one looking after her?

Me! That's who. I can try and get her well, but if we send her back out to be a pawn for fun again, she will slip back into a stressful state of mind. It won't be good for her in the long run!

You saw what she did last night, well tried too, Sebastian and she also went off into the frozen wasteland on her own and she doesn't even realize she did! She doesn't understand me when I told her about it." Owen yells.

"Owen, we don't ever send pawns home and remember the agreement we have going right now. We let her go, we'll be screwing ourselves over." Hadrian grumbles.

"And staying here will kill her like it did to Dana. Look, I think we should send her and Her friends home. It would save us pain, time and effort. Julius is using us as pawns and we'll just come back next time. You and Rain are somewhat untouchable and you love me, Harriet and Rain to much to let us go and if neither of you want to agree to my plan, then I will take care of Valerie here in our home, sparing no expensive on the resources it uses, get her well enough to walk and I will take her and her friends back to where they belong myself."

Before I know it, they're all arguing and Shelby is getting very upset in the corner. "Oh, look what you have done, Owen! You've upset your sister!" Sebastian yells and I see Rain gently help Shelby to her feet, Declan in her arms.

"Shelby, baby, why don't you go to your room and rest? I will come see you in a bit, okay?" Rain urges slowly and she nods, carrying Declan away without so much as word.

"Bye, daughter!" I hear Sebastian call out and he gives a half hearted, gentle, 'bye' to her.

I feel Ricky grip my arm, pulling me back to hide from Shelby behind the door as she leaves the room. I sware Declan is looking at me and Ricky. He knows, but why isn't he sorting out any mess? Something seems off this time... It's like his scared of standing up or something.

Ricky moves a finger to his lips and Declan stays quiet. "Come on, we've seen enough." He says, lifting me up carefully to carry me back to my room.

As we hurry back to the room I came from, I notice another room with a bed and the person in it is, sitting at the edge of the bed clutching their head, tears falling. "S-Sam...!" I choke out and Ricky sees this, but is more concerned for me and keeps running before she can notice us... She's awake! And he looks deeply saddened.

Chapter 22

'm still trying to process alot of stuff in my mind. Then...
A memory tugs at me from under the surface. I see my
hands reaching into a cupboard at the small house, turning
a core ball over. I stole it? How badly did I want to go back
home subconsciously? Has it be confiscated from me or have
I hidden it somewhere?

I shrug my shoulders and then I feel power flowing through
my fingers. It starts of small, but a small ball of light is there.
I concentrate on it hard, my powers are still here? And then
left behind is the core ball in my hands. It's pretty 'weighty' in
my hands and I try to activate it, but nothing happens. I give
up after some time, sigh and manage to make it vanish, but I
can feel it's near and within my reach somehow, unavailable
to others.

I flinch when I hear my door creaking open. It's Shelby and
she's not wearing her mask. She looks tired and puzzled, only

sort of just peeking in. "Hello?" I whisper hoarsely and I see her jump back a little, but she doesn't outright leave.

"M-Morning..." She whimpers back in a kind of childish voice. Her hands are fidgeting, eyes darting all over the place. "Can I help you?" I ask feeling like she might not be a threat to me...

I see her shoulders rise and slump, then she pushes a strand of her dyed hair behind her ear. "Where's Declan? His usually with you..." I tell her.

"His sleeping." She answers, not giving me much to go on. She's not very talkative is she? Hell... She's usually pretty 'aggressive', but this girl before me now hardly seems the same as the girl I met before... wait, I've been pretty 'out of it' according to Owen and living a different outcome! Maybe her entire persona is different this time around?

"What's the weather like this morning?" I ask. I see she perks up a-bit at me asking a 'proper' question. "It's cold, Father said we might get a bit of a blizzard today." She responds, cracking a small smile. I smile back to her which seems to make her happy. Then I hear a door opening and closing followed by some foot steps. Her eyes go wide and she darts into my room, gently closing the door, but keeping an eye out.

I hear another door open and close a second and later. She seems to breathe a sigh of relief and turns around, looking at me. "Do you..." She trails off.

"Do I what?" I ask.

"Wanna play?" She smiles, her eyes lighting up. Should I be trusting this girl?! She has her hand out for me to take. "Father doesn't have to know. 15 minutes? I never have anyone to play with in here! You're the first girl my age I've seen in here!" She tells me, clapping her hands.

"Sherbet, I-I don't know if I'm really allowed to leave this room..." I tell her.

"If anyone asks, I'll cover for you!" She smiles, still holding out her hand. I roll my eyes and give in. "Alright, what's the worst that could happen?" I say, throwing the sheets back and placing my pillow to be 'me' and then covering it up again. "Yay!" She squeals, grabbing my hand and pulling me outside the room and down the hall, but not before us both gently closing the door of my 'room'.

I take a breath in as I'm sitting on a bright pink bean bag in her room that pretty much looks like a child's... She's inside some kind of, 'pop-up' tent, colouring in a colouring book and her legs kicking back and fourth as she focuses. I sigh and rest my face in my hand, turning my head to look at her bed. It's fairy themed.

Declan is on it, curled up sleeping, his tail moving every so often. I look back to Shelby. She's now humming a song and a crayon rolls out of her hand. I pick it up and hand it to her. She begins to thank me when she stops mid-sentence, looks frightened beyond belief, drops the crayon and she's pushing herself away from me, looking like she's about to burst into tears.

"W-what! H-how! How! What are you doing in here?! Where am I?! What's going on?!" She yells at me and I jump to my feet, backing towards the door. "W-what do you mean?! Y-you are the one who brought me in here!" I respond and I see Her eyes widen. "I-I did?!"

"Yes!" I yell back. She looks sad now and then looks back up to me with anger. "Get. Out. Valerie." She growls and I nod, accepting the situation for what it is and pull the door open to step outside, ignoring her. She's cursing about the pinkness of the room, then squeals just as I feel a hand on my shoulder.

I gulp.

I turn around slowly to look and now I see Shelby is hiding back in the tent again, she's rocking back and fourth, holding Declan with a tear streaked face. He lets out a small, sad 'meow'.

"It's okay, Sherbet... You just hide in there. Valerie won't hurt you one bit, I promise, she's harmless, but I do need to get her back to her room though."

I see she's glaring, but it's not at me and starts crawling out of the tent.

I relax that it's just Owen and I look at him. He gives me a somewhat 'annoyed' look. Yikes! "Come on, let's go." He says without a bit of empathy and he forcefully drags me out of the room, leaving a puzzled Shelby behind.

Owen brang me back to my bed and now his taking my pulse. "Valerie" He says pretty casually.

"Yes...?"

"Why did you disturb, Sherbert?" He says, looking up. You can see his warm, honey brown eyes.

"I didn't, she approached me."

"Oh, I see... Apologies for blaming you then."

"Owen, why was she... Different?"

"She's been through alot in the past, Valerie... I feel perhaps it's best if you leave our pasts alone."

"S-sorry!"

"Don't blame yourself, it's not your fault to begin with."

And then he let's go, placing my wrist down again. "Owen..." I say.

"Yes, Valerie?" He answers, pulling off latex gloves and disposing of them.

"When can I leave and go back to my fiends?"

"Valerie-"

"Please, you can't keep me here! I want to see them!"

"I know you want to see them, but it's my job to make sure you're going to be okay. How much worse can a few days be? I haven't been 'totally unbearable' have I, Valerie?" He says getting a little grumpy with me.

I nod slowly and back down. "No, you haven't been."

"Thank for for your reasonability, Valerie."

I sigh. "Is there anything I can get you?" He asks me.

"No, I just want to be left alone, Owen.."

"Alright, I will respect that. Afternoon tea should be in a few hours." He says and I nod watching him turn around, pack up a his medical kit. I pull the blankets up and turn my head feeling that my eyes are tired and heavy. "Do you mind if I rest a bit?" I murmur out.

"Not at all! You go right ahead, Valerie" I hear him answer while sorting through something. About two minutes later, I hear a voice.

"Son."

"Owen, sweetie."

"Mother, Father? What are you doing here?!"

"Something- I- I mean,

we

should have done a long time ago."

"And what is that, Father?"

"Prevent you from getting in

our

way of course my 'dear', 'darling', Owen just like the daughter who abandoned us before did." Rain whispers.

"What in Kiki's name are you both talking about?! She didn't abandon you! She let you go because if you love someone, you let them go. She wanted you to learn some lessons to one day return home! And can you not see I'm just as busy as you both?! I'm afraid that I have Valerie to be looking after."

"Oh, really? Well, allow me, us to take her off you're hands for you."

"You will do

NO

such thing!"

"Really? Because... I think we already have, Son.
"

And Sebastian clicks his fingers.

"Rain"

"Mother, what the hell?! Step away from her!"

"I'm afraid that you're not in charge of her 'care' anymore, Owen. She's valuable, elite, a real diamond in the rough."

"Father, your talking is nuts and frankly, you haven't made any sense in centuries! Mother, I will not ask you again! Step away from my patient, Valerie."

"You're time is over, Son."

"Father-"

And I squeeze my eyes shut, hearing the sound of a gun-shot and a body falling to the ground.

I jolt awake, hearing a scary sound. Was I just having a weird, loud dream? The room is blurry and bathed in light blue hues and grey tones. Slowly it's coming to a stand still, all normal colour returning. "Owen!" I call out, hoping that his not too far away, but what I see is horrible...

Owen is laying on the floor, groaning, heavily bleeding and clutching his stomach, hissing in pain. I gulp seeing Sebastian there and his straightening out his tie and smoothing out wrinkles in his clothing. My eyes widen.

"So glad, I didn't get get a drop of blood on my nice, clean, pressed uniform." He says boldly, ignoring my consciousness completely. "Sebastian?!" I yell out, hoping to get his attention. He turns his head looking at me and then ignores me again.

"Sebastian, what did you do?!" I try again. "Shut up, Sprout!" He growls.

"Ah-ah, I don't think so!" I scold.

"Well, I think it's time you settled down now, Valerie. I'm, oh so glad that we had this chat and that doesn't mean just you, sweetie-pie."

I gulp and turn my head seeing her. I feel her grip my wrist roughly.

"Let go!" I cry weakly, trying to pull my arm away, but she doesn't let go. "Hurry it up, wifey. Enough, 'dilly dallying!'" I hear Sebastian comment who has his hands behind his back and is just turned away from us, waiting.

"Rain, you don't have to do this!" I beg her, struggling. I see she has a needle ready. "Rain! Please don't do this! You're better than this, I know it and inside, you know it too!" I cry again and she gives me one shake of the head and I feel a sharp slight pain.

Soon enough, the world is fading to black and I can hear their gentle chuckles. "W-why didn't you just let us go home? Let me go home..." I cry out weakly and unable to do anything.

"No chance, Sprout. No chance while I'm still alive, my heart beating." I hear Sebastian laugh. "And now you're both down & out too." Rain adds on. Then it's all over.

Chapter 23

Two voices cut through the silence. I'm unable to will my eyes to open. "When should she wake up, honey?"

"Any time now, baby. Let's deal with Avery while we wait for our newest prize to add to our collection of Elite to wake up."

"Good idea, baby! This is why I love you! You're so smart!"

"And I love you my baby ."

Yuck! I can feel myself wanting to gag upon hearing their conversation, but I can't.

I hear a door open. "Sebastian, Rain!"

"What is it, Paige? You know that you and other Guards aren't allowed in here! This is our private laboratory!"

"I'm aware of that, sir. It's important though."

"Spit it out, Paige! I and Sebastian don't have all the time in the world."

"Uh..."

"Oh, wait, yes we do! Ha, but just not in this timeline as we'll reach old age, but we'll respawn so to speak considering our daughter doesn't want us to leave this cycle."

"I-I know. Y-yes, Miss. I-I understand. It's just that Ricky has gone on a slight rampage and gone missing, the two last remaining members of Avery's and Sam's team are gone too...

W-we secured the rest of Valerie's team in the the exiled section of the city. They're pretty upset at us which is under-standable a-and S-Sam became emotional when she heard that, Ricky had gone missing. She's gone... Like, well, I don't know. Almost like she's in a coma again...

Why did you have to shoot Owen-"

"Shut up, Paige! I'll come deal with the whole shitstorm, alright?"

And then Rain leaves, following Paige. "Well, Avery. You've been graced for a few more minutes. Let's just give you another sedative to prolong your sedation even though we already have you under. Wouldn't want you waking up on us again while were not ready for you.

Hmm, I should check on Shelby and see how she is while were having a little 'sidetracking.'

See if she's ready..." And then I hear Sebastian's feet trail away, the door closing behind him. I try to strain, but I can't break whatever is holding me down and then I feel myself lapse into unconscious again.

-

--

I wake up hearing voices and the sound of stuff being moved around. "Geez, she isn't awake yet?"

"Seems not, Rain. We must have injected too much."

"Hmm... Maybe."

"You should have known better!"

"Me? Excuse me? How dare you!"

I feel an itchy feeling in my Nose and I scrunch my face up. I let out a shaky breath and next thing I know is the sound of footsteps. "Ah, good. You're awake!"

Was that Sebastian? I peel my eyes open. Everything is blurry, but it's enough to make out him and her, towering over me. They have lab coats on and masks across their face. Rain's long hair is pinned up in a bun.

"Come on, Sprout, don't keep us waiting." Sebastian hisses. I shake my head, trying to clear my fog. I also give a kick or two, but as I'm still restrained down. It's no use.

"You aren't getting out of that so easily, Valerie." Sebastian says. "What have you done?!" I cry. "Owen was your son! Why are you doing all this stuff to everyone? Let me go!" I cry which earns me a light slap from Rain. It stings a little, but not a whole lot as I'm still under the influence of medication.

"Let us tell you something, Valerie." Sebastian says, pulling a seat over for him to sit on. Rain too.

"W-what?" I choke out.

"I'm so sick of people getting in my way. I-I mean o-our way." Sebastian shudders when Rain glares at him. "This community is supposed to be a nice place to live, but without followers, it's not so nice. You're ruining our community that we've worked hard to build, stressing them out, some are rebelling because of you and your friends and you've dragged Avery, Samantha and the 'guys' down with you too."

I think you could do better, be elite. In time, I suppose you'll make better decisions then." Sebastian snickers, Rain does too. "Now, let's kick-start the process, hmm, Sprout? I know You have potential, we just need to bring it out don't we?"

Him and Rain stand up from their seats. Rain pulls a cart towards them. A tray is on it filled with about seven syringes. They are all white and look like they just came out of the freezer except for the last one which is a light, murky blue. It does look slightly frozen though... I see Rain and Sebastian pull on some surgical gloves and they both pick up a white needle each.

"W-what is that? What are you going to do to me?!" I cry out. "Not you, Sprout. Not now anyway, but soon." Sebastian responds as they both look at me while holding a needle each in their Hand.

I feel a few tears start to slide down my face and I let out a small whimper, lightly tugging and pulling on my restraints when I hear a unexpected Voice. "V-Valerie?"

I turn my head and try to sit up as best I can. Avery is awake and sitting up as best she can too despite her restraints. "Aw, shit." I hear Sebastian curse. "Does it really matter now? Don't worry about her being awake. It will just cause her to suffer more simply and I don't mind if Valerie hears. Might assist in breaking her if anything and hearing both their screams could be quiet pleasant!" Rain says.

"Maybe you're right, maybe you're onto something." Sebastian says. I see them both head over to Avery. She's cowering in fear with both of them on either side of her. "V-Valerie?" She chokes out, her eyes bug wide. "Just be good Avery and this will all be over with so much faster." Sebastian says and I see him and Rain both pull tighter on the last of Avery's restraints that she's held more firmly against the bed. She has her head turned and looking right at me.

"She can't help you, Avery." Sebastian taunts. "W-why are you doing this? Stop, Please!" She cries out, but they ignore her and then I see them both inject their needles into both her shoulders, each. She cries out, screaming and is trying to move writhe around, but she can't.

"Just close your eyes, Avery! It w-willbe over s-soon! Y-you can just drift away..." I choke out as it's the only thing I can think of. "Y-you'll see Sam!" I say, not having the heart to tell her that Samantha is still alive. They were all tricked, everyone into still thinking Samantha was dead.

This way she will have something to look forward too, I hope she's not angry with me in death...

"VALERIE!" She screams much louder when they inject her with a 3rd and 4th needle. They step back and I see Avery start to convulse a little, but it stops quickly. She hasn't vomited luckily, but her pupils are enlarged though...

"Last ones." Rain says, grabbing the another needles. One white one is left for me. I-Is that one left for me? I hope not, but I know I'm wrong. It's just wishful thinking...

"V-Valerie..." I hear Avery whimper. She's still looking at me. I see a tear slide down her cheek, her face and skin turning sickeningly pale. "I'm sorry, Avery. I love you." I utter. She tries to speak, but can't and I see her eyelids flutter, then they close completely. Her chest is no longer rising and I see Sebastian and Rain both take a step back away from her.

"W-why?!" I yell out. They ignore me. They're really quick to shuffle her into a body bag and throw onto the floor like she's trash. I scrunch my eyes up, feeling them burning and resisting the urge to be sick. My hands shake as I scrunch them up, feeling tingly.

If only I had my powers...

I hear the sound of metal and I open my eyes.

"W-why did you do this?! WHY?!" I yell out, choking on my tears. I almost choke fully. Dying on my tears would be better than being here..."You know why. Now for you, miss diamond though, a scuffed up one right now. But like we believe, we can shape you into what you're truly supposed to be, elite and Avery? She was just another one of the hundreds of members we have.

All useless." Sebastian says. I see him pick up the last white needle. "W-what is it going to do?! What is it?!" I cry.

"Merge in it's converted form, except this is extra strength as we combined it with some other medicine. You will having a convulsion or two, but we have an antidote. Let's just make you a little more susceptible rather than forgetting who you are now, hmm?" Sebastian says,

"Forgetting who I am?" I ask, and then I let out a scream feeling Rain pull on the restraints to hold me down more firmly. I scream again louder, feeling the burn from the needle as Sebastian injects me.

A painful agonizing 10 minutes by. They're smirking at me, watching me suffer. My voice is hoarse from screaming and my eyes are truly burning. I can feel the dry tears on my Face. W-why aren't I dead yet?! Why?! I'd rather die than endure this fate! This isn't destiny.

I suppose not though because I've only had one needle of the stuff. Avery was given five in the space of two minutes. Is this how Sam felt when she fell in a lake contaminated by Merge and I left her for dead? I'm so selfish!

I let out a cough, feeling something disgusting on me.. Someone wipes it off.

"That's one convulsion and one near convulsion, Sebastian. We let this go on any longer and she may die or end up brain damaged..." I hear Rain utter. "Fine, fine. Let's give her the Antidote now." Sebastian says. I feel a needle in my arm and it's feels like I'm getting drowsy. I force my eyes open and everything is blurry. I look at them before blacking out again. Not without hearing one sentence though.

"Congratulations Valerie, you're no longer a Sprout or a scuffed up diamond. You're elite, all nice and shiny!" Sebastian bellows.

Chapter 24

Feeling different, not myself is disconcerting for me.

Whatever happened to me after I passed out, left me awake, but locked into my body and unable to voice my opinion, nor argue. I'm not in control. I woke up on this chair and have been alone for hours until just now. Sebastian and Rain are in the room, they're office. They're standing by his desk, looking out the window at the Community as the sun rises, but that doesn't help make anything less cold.

I don't think anything's going to be getting better now for me, only worse or my friends for that matter. Where are my friends?

Sam's back to being out of action while Owen and Avery are dead and I know that for a fact, my friends fate is unknown, just that they were carted off, Harriet ran away or something with some random guy from the the exiled section of the city accompanied by some hologram and Shelby Brown... I honestly don't know entirely.

I hear a set of footsteps and a person stops right in-front of me. I blink my eyes upon seeing her., Shelby! She's dressed up in a slightly girly attire than I've ever seen her wear and her hair is into pigtails, but her face is stern.

She gently pokes me in the nose with the tip of her finger, saying 'boop!' and then she slaps me, letting out a slight maniac laugh and places her hands on her hips, grinning. Sebastian and Rain haven't noticed this. What is she playing at?! I can tell she's more like her normal self, but she's faking being different? If I could scoff at her right now, I would.

"Well, you're certainly different this morning. Nothing like the girl who's screams kept me awake last night!" She hisses. "Sherbet!" Sebastian scolds, turning around, his hands behind his back. Rain strides over to Shelby, pulling her away from me slightly.

"Sorry, Mummy and Daddy." Shelby pouts.

"Oh, it's alright our angel, but just be careful with her, I don't want her face bruised up or any part of her for that matter." Sebastian states. "Sorry, I won't do it again." Shelby adds on. apologizes, looking hurt. They reassure her it's okay, Sebastian patting her hair with his hand.

"So, any word on Harriet from the Guards?" Sebastian speaks up. "No, sissy's just gone." Shelby responds, twirling the end of her pigtail with her finger and her foot moving around.

"She's really not worth it, Sebastian. We chased her once, let's just her leave if that's what she wants to do. Maybe she'll come crawling back to us next time?" Rain suggests to him rather snappily.

Sebastian let's out a grunt and turns to face me. "How are you doing this morning?" He asks, holding a hand out which he quickly pulls away. "Oh, right! You're locked in there and can't shake my hand!" He laughs, taunting me.

"But I know that you understand every word I'm saying, huh, Valerie?" He says with a sly grin before standing up straight. "Right, I want the Guards to get everything ready. Go tell them to make the arrangement. By noon tomorrow, we will have the one game we've been building up too, just with less contestants than we planned on initially...." He says walking away from me.

"Because I say so and you, Valerie will be our winner!" He says quickly, turning around, spooking me, but I can't flinch or anything. It's really uncomfortable and even hurts. It's like an itch I can't scratch.

And then they all burst into laughter in-front of me. "Come on, let's go prepare ourselves some breakfast. You can go change, Shelby. We need you out on the field with the Guards." Rain tells her which she nods at, excitedly that she's pleasing them.

"What about her?" Shelby asks, looking in my direction. "Oh, don't worry about her. It's not like she can go anywhere. Till I want her to go somewhere that is." Sebastian snickers and they flick the chandelier above, off and slam the door shut behind them of their office, leaving me alone, paralyzed with just thoughts for company and my inner-most thoughts right now?

I hate them all and I want them dead after everything they've done to me and more importantly my friends and others that I've come to call my friends here.

Chapter 25

"Why would they lock us in here?" The two guys from Sam's team asked, looking up who are sitting on the other-side of the room, not too far away from Kelsey and Cloud. "Obviously because they're going to hurt us! Or something else!" Louis shouts at them before he stands up and starts kicking the door again.

"Luis, stop doing that! You will only hurt yourself. God, just sit down, we're goanna have to wait this out. There is no plan B, and what has gotten into you all of a sudden? Your behavior has been... erratic. You're heading down a slippery slope, one similar to what Valerie's been going through." Cloud scolds him.

"And we've been here for days since Valerie attempted to take her life! We don't know if she's okay or even alive. The leaders must be planning something if they locked us up in this tiny room after they separated us from, Valerie." Louis responds as the guys from Sam's team look around at the small, square claustrophobic room they've been in for days. No windows, a solid door that they can't hear anything outside of and a small light that only just illuminates the room on the roof.

Luis takes a seat, his stomach rumbling. "Do you think they will feed us soon?"

"Soon, I'd imagine. We've lost all track of time, but they have been feeding us before-hand though so why would they stop?" One of the guys pipe up. "What time do you think it is?" Louis responds, staring at the stupid light that's been on the whole time they've been locked up.

The guys shrug while Cloud doesn't say anything, hugging Kelsey closer to him who's been incredibly quiet, almost catatonic. "How's she doing?" Luis asks, turning to face his friend.

"Not good. She hasn't spoken a single word since we were thrown in here. You know that, Louis. I am really concerned about Kelsey's welfare right now, this isn't good. She's barely moved too. The most she does is eat and drink as she just stares blankly, but it's rather slowly." Cloud tells him.

"Kelsey?" Luis whispers gently, taking her hand in his palm, cupping his other hand over her hand that has started shaking. "Kelsey, are you in there?"

Only one small tear manages to find it's way and slides down her face from her eyes as she doesn't say a word back to him, only gently lowering her head as she leans onto Cloud's lap who lets her lay down and he gently presses a hand against her forehead.

"No fever." Cloud says. "Are you tired, Kelsey?"

She gives a weak nod and Louis removes his jumper off, draping it over her as a blanket because she's lightly shivering, their room with a mild tinge to it. "I... I..." She manages to croak out, her voice rather quiet. "You what?" Louis asks, moving to sit closer to her as he continues holding her shaking hand in his and begins to rub her knuckles comfortably with his thumb.

"I want to see, Valerie. Where is she?" She manages to ask, her eyes widening a little. Louis doesn't say anything, not knowing what to tell her and she gently pulls her hand out of his, bringing it to her chest. "Why don't you rest a-bit, Kelsey?" Cloud urges gently, playing with her long blonde pig-tails. She nods slowly and closes her eyes, taking a small breath in before breathing out as she falls asleep to the others relief. Food is shoved into their prison not long after through a small hatch in the bottom of the door which they all eat quietly.

Kelsey manages a few bites despite being woken up by them, she's a little grouchy and that's it before she rejects what Cloud is offering her, not wanting anymore. Hours pass and the food has since been devoured with the empty bowls and plastic utensils to prevent them hurting themselves sitting off the side when Luis lets out a half hearted scream, falling onto his back as he was sitting against the door, some-one having fully opened it. He looks up, his vision blurring to see Ricky standing there, looking upside down.

"Sebastian and Rain are ready for you all. Come along."

They all stand up slowly, going with him. There rest of the other Guards are there also to prevent any of them escaping. "Is she okay?" Ricky asks, raising an eyebrow as he sees how slow Kelsey is walking, just taking tiny steps as Cloud practically supports her entire weight so she doesn't topple over as she's clinging to him, her hands shaking.

"No, of course not! hat do you think? Louis hisses at him, sarcastically which he just ignores before going back to escorting them all, outside into the cold, harsh winter world beyond the gates of the Community...

Shelby sits on the floor of her bedroom inside her tent, Declan beside her, curiously tilting his head as he watches her flip through a scrapbook of happy and sad memories documented by photographs and mementos.

"Declan?" She whispers, no longer bothering to turn the pages of it anymore. She tugs at a tutu like skirt she's wearing, scowls at the childish shirt she has on, pulls a necklace of plastic daisy shaped beads off of her neck and kicks the ballet flats shoes she's wearing off her feet and pulls the bright colorful elastics bunched around her pigtails out.

"Meow." Declan worries, looking up at her and she slowly strokes his ears with her hand.

"This feel alien to me." She tells him.

"Meow."

"Uh, allow me to elaborate... I... Don't belong here. This isn't my world. I don't know how it happened, but things here are different from what I last remember. Everything is like the total opposite almost of what should, I mean did happen and I'm...

Look at how I'm dressed, look at this room. This isn't my life, I'm not this me version of me. I don't recognize any of the stuff in this book. Who I am supposed to be? I've crossed dimensions somehow and I don't understand... I touched Valerie's hand and then, bam! I was awake, I was me.

If I try to tell Sebastian and Rain, they won't believe me."

"Meow?"

"They're not my real parents, Declan. They're just... Pretending they are, pretending I'm their real child. Everything they do is a game of pretend, although I guess they're not the only ones pretending right now and here."

"Meow..."

"You're a good listener you know? You always have been."

"Meow!"

"Aw, so cute! Who's a sooky cat that I love so much?" Shelby giggles and Declan crawls into her arms and snuggles into her chest. "That's right, you are!

Uh, anyway... I've been thinking... Valerie, Kelsey and Louis are just like 'Mother and Father' and... I resent them as well. They're evil, they're... Witches & Wizards? I don't know what they are and I'm younger than Brother and Sister was. I've always felt treated younger, not equal.

I don't know what's going on exactly, but I have a feeling this has Valerie written all over it. Actually..." She says, standing up hurriedly and heading to a mirror, looking at girly, doll-like appearance as opposed to her normal style, punky, maybe even a little spunky, edgy, gothic, tomboyish, grungy look just like Harriet. It's one of the things they had in common before, the same dress sense.

Someone she had and still does look up to even if she doesn't have it in her to tell Harriet that she still loves her like a Sister despite their past differences and difficulties in their relationship.

"I'm going to get revenge, I'm going to take Valerie down and I will correct this incorrect destiny. For I am Sherbert and I will do whatever it takes to succeed. I do not back down from obstacles!" She says confidently, wiping away a tear before it can fall and she picks up a hairbrush, then throwing it at the mirror, causing it to shatter.

Shelby turns around and strides straight to her bedroom door. They'll be in for a shock, but they have their powers so she'll never be at risk of harm or even death. "Mother, Father, I would like to talk!" She calls down the hall, leaving her room and more importantly, Declan behind.

"Julius, I hate you." He speaks up, his voice coming out human rather than in a series of meows.

"Feelings mutual, Declan, but may I remind you who's really in control here? Me and you're a pathetic cat." A voice says from thin air.

"Not always, Julius. Not always."

"Ha, I'd like to see that!"

"Then just you wait. There is more to a story than the meets the eye. Always."

"I'm waiting then. Surprise me, Declan! You have my full attention!" The voice laughs and Declan sprints out of the room on his four legs, going after his owner and one true love, Shelby.

Chapter 26

"**J**ust waiting for everyone else to show up." Sebastian responds, clapping his gloved hands together as a small cloud leaves his mouth, mixing with the chilly air.

A simple fence lines at the edge of the lake, outlining it's perimeter and in the distance, I can see a few of the Guards heading our way. I can't believe were doing this and even more shocking is that Sebastian and Rain are allowing their 'daughter' to compete. Do they NOT care about her safety in compacity?! Oh, I am kidding asking such a dumb question!

And then I wince, feeling my mind clear up, losing my thoughts. Whatever they have me on has turned me into a mindless zombie somewhat. That's how right now feels.

"I hope you're ready, *******!" Rain snickers. "Let's do this! You've got my back, got it?" Shelby snaps at me. She's smirking darkly. Why, what did I ever do to her really? I let out a light groan of pain, feeling the muscles in my stomach contract and Sebastian swats me harshly on the uppper back.

"Go, Valerie. Bring a victory home, why don't you?" He says. Why would I do that for them? Wait... My name is Valerie? My mind feels jumbled, it's like I'm forgetting some stuff.

Feeling an itch climb up my body that turns into almost a burning sensation, I take a step forward that I can't control, ignoring the heavy clunkiness of the armour I'm wearing and pull out an old sword from a sheaf attached to my waist, moving into a 'ready' stance. Shelby and the few Guards do the same.

"No unfair fighting, tricks or weapons beyond the medieval time period. Those are the rules! And we'll be watching." Sebastian announces. Looking ahead of me, I see three young men, one young woman and an old man. I don't recognize them.

"Well, go on!" Speaks up a Guard that's not playing and standing off to the side. He harshly shoves our opponents onto the frozen lake and they're weapons look worse off than ours and they haven't been given any armour at all. Looking around me, I bite my lip.

Is this a trap? It has to be, I'm the one on here with by far the heaviest armour. My team-mates have armour, but it's more modern than mine.

I see Rain and Sebastian close a wooden gate and take a seat on two conventionally placed ice thrones to spectate. "What is this?" Two young men say together, shaking. "I think they want us to fight each-other..." The older man trails off. "Perhaps to the death?"

"No, no, no! Were not doing that, not out here!" The third young man says.

"Oh, well I guess you'll just be losing alot sooner than you or I expected." Rain laughs from the side, her and Sebastian grinning with their arms crossed.

I see the same young man mouth a silent 'fuck you!' which Rain just scoffs at, ignoring him and then one of the guards land a hit at one of the guys on the other team who speak similar, but he blocks and unfortunately is knocked back slightly, stumbling onto his butt as a result and hears a small 'crack' sound beneath his foot. He looks down with worry and then to all his friends.

"Is this some kind of sick joke?" The same young man to swore at Rain speaks up. "You tell us, sprout." Sebastian responds.

"Oh and by the way, this Ice has magical properties. Thought you'd like to know. You fall in there, you'll die. Merge contaminating it will be the least of your concerns, believe me." Rain taunts.

"What, so were to expect today to be our death day?" The same young man shouts which earns a small 'mhmm.' from Sebastian and Rain together.

"I'm going to enjoy slaughtering you all!" Ricky laughs, but I can tell it's forced. I don't think he wants to be mean and the other two guys across from us who speak similar drop their weapons, hugging each-other in panic. "Come on, move! Don't just stand there!" The third young man demands. demands.

"W-we can't do this!" They both choke out, scared. The guards role their eyes and ignore them for later as they will be easy pickings clearly. "Oh, what fun this is going to be fishing their bodies out afterwards, Rain!" Sebastian laughs. "Or we could just not?"

Which him and Rain both erupt into laughter together. The Guards, including Ricky and Paige with I and Shelby start closing in on the young man who's been blatantly rude plus the old man and the only female on their team. "Come on, Kelsey! You have to move!" The old begs, trying to pull a young girl to move, but she only shakes her hand desperately, tears running down her face and doesn't move. A small ice snapping sound sounds causing concern to run through the young man and old man who meet each others glance and the old man shakes his head.

"She isn't well enough for this, I won't be able to get her to move, Louis and if I carry her, we'll fall through the ice in a single spot as it will be double the weight!" The old man lectures as right now, they're all slightly spread out.

"Just try, Cloud! I'll do my best to hold them off. We did learn Karate in Solayo's class, although we weren't into any intense stuff so don't judge my skills!" This 'Louis' says, stepping up to Paige in which he just gulps, not moving into a defensive stance, eyes widening while 'Kelsey' remains kneeling, eyes closed. "Kelsey, you have to move it! Do you hear me right now? If you don't, then you're going to die here! Do you want that? We'll fall through the Ice. I either help you or I leave you, make your choice now because we don't have much time." 'Cloud' says sternly in which she slightly opens her tear stained eyes, looking up at him.

"Valerie may not be Valerie anymore, but she'd want you to go on, right? You're a fighter, not a quitter according to her. She's always believed in you even when you didn't believe in yourself and I know what you're capable of! I'd hate to leave you here and even worse, witness your death. I don't want to leave you to die here, Kelsey! You have a brighter future ahead of you, you're full of potential! All of you are!

You, Louis and Valerie have been like my children right now and everything we've been through so far only makes that feeling inside of me only grow stronger with every passing day."

She slowly nods her head and climbs to her feet with his help who pulls her forward quickly just as a large zone of ice breaks, water enveloping slightly. Sweat is running down her forehead, her eyes widened as she looks at the spot where they just were. I look to Rain and her hand is up slightly and is bright blue. She's cheating, they're cheating!

This is rigged! They're using their powers to manipulate this game! What happened to the rules such as, playing fair?!

"Ouch!" Screams Louis which scares Kelsey. "Louis!" She screams, seeing him hit the ice on his butt, a nasty cut down his arm that was done by a dagger, Paige is holding. She steps back and I run up, sliding in-between her and Louis and raise my sword.

He tries his best to edge away from me. "No, no, no! Please no! Marlie, it's me, Scout. I know you're in there somewhere. This isn't you, you don't want to hurt me do you?

We have alot to talk about and I want to get us and our friends out of here so we can all talk. I don't know what Sebastian and Rain did to you or why I can recall memories from another world and timeline, but stop! I'm your friend and so is Kelsey and Cloud.

You don't want to hurt us."

What is he talking about? I don't understand!

I take a deep breath in, feeling by bottom lip jostle and then I feel light-headed. A slight pain radiates through my skull, a few memories coming unlocked. I know what his saying makes sense, they are my friends, but for someone reason this murderous feeling is inside of me and no matter how much I don't want listen too it, I can't tune it out.

But our names aren't Scout and Marlene. I'm Valerie and his, Luis!

"Valerie, snap out of your head. We fucking need you right now!" I hear Shelby scold me. She looks really distressed. I manage to fight to clear my head a little more and I hear Sebastian yell at me, standing up from his seat.

"Go on, Valerie! They aren't your friends, fight them. Do it, Sprout. Like yesterday!"

I nod and position my sword for Louis when I see tears slide down his face and he slowly lowers his head, closing his eyes, just waiting for me to stab him right through the heart when I hear another voice echo in my head. One that's familiar, but I can't pick who, telling me to just wait one moment if I can and then I let out half a yelp feeling Louis grip the handle of m sword , yanking it from my hand that is slides across the ice.

"Bro, really?! God, you're pathetic, Valerie!" I hear Shelby grow, taking her anger out on me and Louis. "Fuck this, I'll finish him then. Dad, you didn't give her enough!" Shelby says, aiming a bow and arrow, advancing on Louis.

He takes one last look at me, having opened his eyes and he mouths a sentence I've been waiting my whole life to hear... Well, not my whole life, but years.

He says

,

"I love you."

This seizes my heart and I feel my hands start to shake. Little bit little, I can flex my fingers of my own accord and I make the decision to run across the ice and retrieve my blade and throw it through the air, straight for Shelby. She screams, stepping away from Louis, the blade right through her shoulder. Louis uses this as his chance to sprint away from Shelby, but not before stealing her bow and he thrusts it to Kelsey who catches it perfectly.

"You monster!" She screams, yanking the sword out of her shoulder, but she collapses to her knees, screaming from the pain, thick, warm blood oozing out onto the ice as she lays there, crying.

"What do we do we?!" I hear the Guards start panicking. "Uh, uh, uh?" Ricky responds, not panicking less hard. "Now! This is our chance!" The two guy's from Louis team call out and they race to the fence, helping each-other over it. "Oh, no you don't!" Sebastian says angrily, racing to his feet and heads straight around the fence's outline to the guy's on the other side with a gun out. They start backing away, looking cornered by Sebastian.

"Okay, I'm halting this!" Rain calls out, raising her hands and they're both glowing brightly. She's going to freeze us all! Damn it, if we only we had our powers! We'd stand a chance at defending ourselves, maybe even fighting back if the stars are on our side. She's heading onto the rink and I feel my breathing increase rapidly.

I clench my hand, just wishing for a miracle when she lets out a scream and I see Declan in his human form out on the ice with us. He teleported in. Well, he took his damn time. He skids past her on the ice.

"Declan?! Where did you come from?! You were locked inside our mansion! You shouldn't be human!" Rain shouts, perplexed. He skids on the ice for a few more seconds and halts perfectly.

"I-It's you... D-Declan, h-help me?" Shelby begs, struggling to speak as her injury becomes aggravated. She reaches her hand out to stroke his cat ears that are on the top of his head. So his a Human-Meifwa hybrid, but also an Angel. Tears in her eyes because fear and panic is building, adrenaline coursing through her veins. He gently extends a hand, helping her up and pulls her close that she's safe in his arms, her clinging to his shirt desperately.

He doesn't even care if she's dirtying up his shirt and he lets her remove his jumper to wrap around her shoulder. He looks me straight into the eyes, I'm able to hear him while he doesn't even open his mouth.

"You weren't supposed to see me before, Valerie. Angel's are supposed to act discretely according to our new code of ethics and rules. I tried to create an illusion so I had time to vanish, but it didn't work due to my weaker than supposed to be powers and you're stronger than your friends.

I can see it, feel it. Your powers never actually vanished and now, the course of history and destiny has been changed due to your interference. This isn't you fault, but in simple terms, you've now influenced the future that James and Julius have written.Well, more messed about with.I know you don't know who they are, but they're both Angels too, paramount to Demons at this point and they're both stronger than you.

Also, Shelby here has been living so many variations of her life and I've spent so much time jumping through all of them, looking for my golden opportunity to save her. I'll keep saving her till I've found every last version of her and now, I'm without much choice in this world as to what's going to happen now that this version of her is dying. If I lose this version, she'll transcend to another timeline which will fracture some key points in time and spaceand increase my workload and me being here in this timeline will have all been for nothing.

Kiki, your God has granted me an emergency clause to use at my discretion. I'm going to bring this Shelby here into her law of cycles now so this isn't all for waste, although I don't know if it will work. I'm not the one in control here and I'll probably ending have to repeat my efforts somewhere along the line.

Never repeat a word of what you've seen here today, please. I beg of you!

Or do, Kiki's always observing. But somehow, I don't think you'll give the Core too much trouble. You'll make a fine Angel yourself one day, but it just won't be with in the happiest of circumstances, but uh - Life is a challenge and suffering isn't forever. You'll meet Kiki and the rest of us, someday.

Were always going to around, we just can't provide an immediate rescue as we'd like too due to power and time restraints, but we'll do our best to help out when we can." He says gently and then he's gone, him and Shelby turning into millions of sparkles. The Guards all look shocked and slowly back away before running off the ice, leaving Ricky and Paige behind.

Rain is mumbling a few words, incoherently before slamming her foot against the ground in anger. "What just happened?! What happened?! No, this can't be!"

"I-I don't know! Don't blame me, as if I know!" Ricky shrugs, running off the ice too and Paige follows him.

"Right, I've had just about enough of you, Valerie. Julius and James are going to be angry that we've broken our deal with them." Rain says angrily, advancing on me. "Deal? What deal?! I don't know anything about a 'supposed deal!'" I cry.

"Leave her alone!" Louis shouts, reaching for Rain and he lands on her, pinning her to the Ice. "Louis!" I say with tears in my eyes. "Let go, you'll fall through the Ice with her!" I cry out, seeing that it's cracking.

"She's right, let go or you'll die too!" Cloud calls out as he hugs Kelsey close in his arms. His almost gotten her off the ice.

Louis lets go and rushes forward, towards me away from Rain who falls through the Ice, vanishing beneath the water.

I look back down to my hand, realizing it's no longer clenched and I see it's shimmering slightly, looking silver.

Rain doesn't resurface and the lake starts too freeze over again. I did that, I just know it. She wasn't expecting me too. I have my powers, they have been here all this time!

But where is Louis and Kelsey's? Have they lost theirs forever?!

Sebastian turns his focus away from shaking the guys from Sam and Avery's team by their collars to see a hole in the Ice. "Rain...?" He gasps, eyes widening and drops the guys onto the snow ground.

"She fell through you, dumb-ass!" Cloud yells at him as he gently edges his way to the edge of the pond and heaves Kelsey up over the fence and then he climbs over afterwards.

"Come on, let's just go, Marlie... I want to talk. I have wanted too for a few days now..." Luis says gently, reaching for my hand, gesturing for me to walk with him to the fence just like Cloud did with Kelsey, but his hand goes straight through my mine, my skin looking somewhat translucent, the sunlight that's streaming going straight through it, my whole body infact that it's all glittering like gold. "I'm not Marlene..." I begin, then we notice the bigger problem at hand.

"What...?" We both say at the exact same time, staring at each-other in horrorat what's just happened.

Chapter 27

W e meet up with the Kelsey and Cloud in which, the guy's from Avery & Sam's team coming running over to us, Sebastian hot on their trail, gun in hand. "Right, that's it! I'm ending you all. I've run out of patience. And you, Valerie were a terrible example of how an 'Elitist' is supposed to behave!"

And then he turns away to look at the frozen over spot that Rain fell through. He shakes his head and I sware I almost see a tear fall from his eye and then he looks up at us, dropping his gun to the snow covered ground.

"I just wanted our family to stay together... The thought of anything coming between of us, I couldn't handle that. I didn't want to lose anyone again, but I keep losing everyone again and again!" He says, looking up at us."Hey sprout, I'm really sorry, okay? To all of you. I'd ask if you guys have it in me to forgive me, but I doubt you would."

He holds out his hand to shake my hand, but my hand just goes through it obviously to his surprise "That's not normal... Or good." He says, gesturing to me and then I see his face pale.

"Julius & James... They're here... Not again, please not again!" He says, dropping to the ground and starts to visibly shake.

"Who are they?" Cloud asks confused. Sebastian starts shaking his head desperately, slapping his hands together in a prayer position as he climbs to his knees, tears truly filling up his eyes. "You don't wanna know, trust me!" He says back shortly."Oh, Daughter, please have mercy! I've learnt my lesson I sware, spare me!"

"HEY!" A voice calls out, we look up to see Owen running towards us with Sam behind him and then we hear laughter ring out. It's Ricky, Sam and Paige together, following Owen.

When they stop, Sam and Ricky share a quick passionate kiss. She looks awful, but standing. They turn to look at Sebastian. "Sebastian, word of advice? Run. I know you killed my other cousin too." Sam says, narrowing her eyes just as Owen approaches us.

"Ah, hi, Son..." Sebastian trails off before seemingly bolting. "Yeah, you better run, 'Dad!'" Owen taunts under his breath, arms folded before he drops them and turns to look at us. "Owen! I-I saw Sebastian and Rain, shoot you!" I cry out which he nods at.

"They did, but it wasn't a fatal shot. Neither of them know how to properly use and aim a gun. I fear for the future though if they learn... I was injured and I'm goanna have to take it real easy for a while though... But I'll be just fine," He trails off.

"Should we go after Sebastian? I wouldn't mind to make him pay." Cloud speaks up. "Nah, let him run, his not worth it... And since when has violence ever solved anything?

Anyway, what did I miss out on?" Owen questions. We glance at the lake and see a wedding ring bobbing in the water.

"A r-ring?" He stammers. "Where's Mum, Harriet and our little Sherbert?"

"Oh, Rain is over there." Cloud points dryly to the bobbing wedding ring. Owen looks shocked, but ultimately doesn't say anything, just accepting it. "And Sherbert and Harriet?" He questions.

"Uh, Shelby vanished? Her stupid cat turned into the human he was, sputtering some nonsense and he left with her into thin air. She was dying." Louis says straight up, shrugging.

"Oh, I see... I know very well who that us. It's better I stay out of their business... Otherwise..."

But Owen doesn't finish this sentence. "And Harriet? I-I can't remember... My memories are patch... I looked for her and couldn't find her..."

My friends shrug and look to me. "Where is Harriet, Valerie?" Kelsey prompts. "She left, with some guy of the same ethnicity to you who was from the exiled portion of the city. Some hologram looking girl showed up too and they all left in a flash of light." I tell.

"Oh, thank the stars! Well, Kiki actually. That is the best possible outcome I could hope for her, but Imageon would be with out all her vital components so it's unknown what kind of state she'll be in, but if Ethan is with both of them then I trust he will look after and watch out for Harriet. He always has."

"Image-on and Ethan?" Louis asks. "Old friends, long story involving Shelby and Harriet somewhat too. Don't ask, I don't wish to re-tell it." Owen responds and then he shoves his hands into his jumper pockets.

"If she's with him then I won't go after her. She deserves to go where she's most happiest and with whoever she wants. Sebastian forced her to stick around here in the end of that story." He shrugs.

"So...What now that Sebastian has escaped?" The guys from Avery and Sam team, stammer.

"Do you all want to go home? I have Sebastian and Rain's Core access control panel. They're reign has gone on for long enough, no point in forcing you all to stick around a place you never wanted to end up in the first place. Come on, follow me. We'll just do it out in the hallway.

Were closer to the Core then." He tells us and we all follow him. He shows a secret way up to the hallway we all first started in, bypassing obstacles.

"I was going to send you all home before when you first showed up here, but Sebastian and Rain didn't want me too. And Sam, Ricky, Paige and Derek and Niall?"

"That's our names!" Our two un-named male friends shriek, jumping around excited.

"I can send you guys home to where you belong too." Owen smiles and then I clutch a hand to my mouth, feeling like I'm going to be sick.

"Are you doing okay now, Valerie? You look sick..." Owen worries.

"Yeah... I'm fine, Owen. Just a little stressed out. Thanks for asking, I'm sorry for the trouble I've caused. I don't know where my head was."

"Oh, it's quiet alright. People can get sick easily in more ways than one. Sebastian and Rain a can have that affect on people. Anyway, I'd advise you all attend your local emergency room though when you return home. Can you promise me that?

I'm sorry for not being more help with your condition, Valerie, and..." But then he trails off.

"Of course, I promise! And you did the best you could" I tell him.

"Well, my best wasn't good enough a 2nd time around." He whispers. "I failed as a Doctor."

"We promise." My friends add on, reassuring him which he smiles at. He holds up the core ball and Sam places her hand on it alongside the guys. So do Ricky and Paige.

"How about you send us to the same place? I frankly never want to see you again, Owen. And if I do, then it'll be too soon." Paige snaps and Ricky nods.

"S-sure... I can do that." He stammers. "Sam?" I say, turning to face her. "What?" She growls.

"I'm sorry about Avery-"

"Don't say it! I just want to forget that any of this happened. Let what's dead or left behind just fade from my memory. The friends I made even if some of them were short lived, the years I've spent here, everything. I'm just thankful I woke up in the end and lived to return home, even if it's with a number of scars and pain.... Bye, Valerie.

It was nice meeting you though, friend." She says, turning to face Owen again. They all vanish into a blinding light and Owen's left standing there, but we can hear their voices, it fading and bouncing around the hallway.

"I hope there's no crop circles, Sam. You told me there was a farmhouse in your family once. I don't like aliens."

"Oh, don't you worry about that! You have me, that's all you should be focused on."

"Yeah?"

"Yeah. Now I wonder how you'll taste slow-cooked. I just need to get my UFO out of my hanger first."

"WHAT?!"

"Hahahaha! Relax, I'm just pulling your leg... Or am I?"

"Don't scare me like that!"

"Just shut up, Ricky and kiss me."

"Oh, okay!"

Then a thought hits me. "The other members of the Community!" I panic. "Oh, I'll release hem all too. They've waited years for this, what will another five minutes hurt?" Owen laughs dryly and we can no longer hear Sam and Ricky talking.

"And you guys?" Owen asks, turning to face the remaining guys of Sam's team.

"Home. We just want to go home. We never came back from our camping trip. It will be mass-panic us walking into the local police station after missing for years, but uh - We need too. Who knows how many family events we've missed?" One of them responds. "Come on, let's go scare the pants off everyone that we've risen from the dead." He says gently, having his friend lean against his shoulder as they place their hand on the ball and vanish too.

"Now, you guys." He says. "Go on, I'm sure your friends are worried sick about you guys. We all holds hand and place our hand on the ball. I can place my hand on the ball, but can't hold my friends hands.

The space around me melds into a bright white and I look up seeing an image infront of me. Louis, Kelsey and Cloud alone, waking up on the floor of the classroom in the dark.

I didn't end up going with them. How, why? They start shouting out and crying my name, running around the room, looking for me.

The commotion they're making, I see the doors to the classroom open and police officers on night duty run in. Before I can listen to what they're saying, the image vanishes and a new voice behind me that I also don't recognize makes the hair on my neck, stick up.

"Ah, welcome Valerie, or should I call you Marlene, aka Marlie? You've just ascended to a higher plain. One that I control where I'm untouchable I like to think. You're not the first of your Valerie who resist me, but ultimately, you never actually resist me.

If you end up dead at my hands, I'll just move onto another timeline. I think I have some use for you though now. There are several more timelines I can touch. I'm not the first Angel to do this and I surely won't be the last. You can't stop shit, Kiki." He laughs. Kiki... There's our God's name.

"Yeah, after the difficult time I've had lately? I'm not going to just become another puppet for someone to toy with to their hearts content, I don't even care who you are. Whatever you have up your sleeve, bring it Mr." I say strongly, turning around to come face to with a guy who's angry.

"Oh, really? Well, bring it on then, Valerie. This all is just one big story to me or a series of story and I'm the author. I write everything at the will of my hand." He says holding up his own Core ball in his hot little hands, tapping it that it lights up.

"Yeah, sure. Let's see about that then. I dare you to bring it." I tell him.

"As you wish, Valerie."

- This Core Access Control Panel has been activated by Angel, Julius -

Accessing world status...

- World status loaded -

<You have imputed a command>

- World status has been re-named to Story chapters -

<You have imputed a command>

- Do you want to write a new timeline? -

<Yes>

New timeline generating now...

- Timeline generated -

- System output

-

Welcome to Destiny, reader. I've been leading you on since you began reading. I made you question every moment something happened, what was real and what was not. I pulled the rug out from under your feet countless times throughout this story and you don't even know the difference. Julius is not who you should fear. His a character and I'M the author.

He doesn't even know I'm leading him on just like we did to Sebastian and Rain.

- You're God, James

Chapter 28

Everyone had either left him, was dead or escaped like a certain man, ex-friend who he hopes he never sees again as long as they both shall live.

Now what is he going to do, alone? Should he jump blindly into another timeline as anywhere would be better than where he is lonely or should he stay alone because it's what he deserves based on his sins to fish Rain's body from the lake and bury it alongside Avery's body next to her dead twin sister and some other friends who are no longer alive.

But his train of thought is interrupted when a pair of foot-steps sound behind him. Whoever it is, they're clearly walking fast, now running to catch up to him.

"Owen! Wait up! Wait up for me!"

He stiffens, the voice familiar. Tears pool in his eyes and he immediately drops the control panel in his arm, not caring about it in the slightest as it hits the ground. He throws his arms around the persons neck and they hug back before both of them let go, stepping away from each-other.

"Harriet... I-I thought you had left, forever again." Owen speaks up.

"Sebastian and Rain should never have dragged you back here in the first place after you ran away the first time, took Julius deal or imprisoned, and locked Ethan up."

"It's all in the past and I was going to run away again, but sometimes some things or friends are more important than others so, I came back for you.

You know what they say about the Core... Every decision has multiple outcomes. Ethan took Image-on back home, my home.

She's been heavily damaged by Sebastian. A-lot of her operating systems aren't operationing or functional.

She's no longer dangerous, but also less 'human' now. His going to check her over, make list of what needs to be repaired and see what he can do for her,

No one there is angry at us for what happened, but I feel for us to apologize anyway to them would be a good idea."

"Yeah, probably for the best. Saying sorry anyway never hurts. So Harriet, why are you here?"

"I told you. I'm here for you. The Core lays out multiple paths for us and later if you want, you could come with me to see Ethan, Image-on and my home could be your home too so you're not here, lonely or ever feeling abandoned."

"I'll think about it..."

"And, Owen? Someone or should I say multiple special individuals want to say, hi. They have a mission for us." Harriet says pointing. Owen slowly turns around and a young woman with brown skin, freckled dotting and long white wavy hair pulled into a ponytail, tied off with a red bow, her eyes purple, complete wit a warm smile, wearing black lace up boots, a black woolen coat with a white dress underneath and perfectly manicured hot pink nails is standing there before them.

"W-who are you?" Owen chokes out. This mysterious woman opens her mouth to reply.

"You can just call me, Kiki. I don't believe in formalities all the time so my complete title isn't necessary. My human name will do just fine.

I called out to Harriet to return back here, but you also matter to her. You both have grown up beside each-other even if you're not biologically related.

I have a job for both of you. Complete it without complaint to the best of your ability and you shall be rewarded.

The Core Control Panel you have there." She says, levitating the ball from Owen's hands slightly who panics an

grasps it. "I want you both to spend some time here in this... Hallway. It's a safe place between worlds, timelines for people. Human or not.

If anyone ever comes through any of these stargate portals or ends up here in unknown way to you, use the control panel to send them to where ever they want to go.

I've made you half-angels for the time being so you can weild the control panel, but I don't want you moving on to develop skills, your appearances altering.

When your task is done, that you both have worked together as a team, I will notify you both and you can leave for your new home.

Now, the Core is very busy as you know so I'll leave you both to it and you can have a bit of a head start.

I have other matters to attend too soon now... See you around, Harrier & Owen." She says walking away from them, hands behind her back, blending into the hallway, a few speckles of glitter left behind.

"Was that-" Owen begins.

"Let's not question it, Owen. We do what were supposed to here and then we can just... leave for our new lives.

There's too much pain here." Harriet whispers.

It's silent between Harriet and Owen. They share a nod and then they hear the sound of a star-gate warping.

A young woman comes stumbling out of it, clothes rather old, tattered and patched, pale as can be with short black hair that is in a ponytail, clearly choppily cut and dull eyes, no life in them.

She is holding a locket in her palm and rests on her hands on her knees, gasping for air. She looks up at them desperately. "I-I'm looking for, Magic's Peak! D-do you know where that is?!" She cries out, asking them as she regains her breath and stands up straight not long after. Owen and Harriet look at each-other.

Harriet giving an encouraging nod to him, Owen slowly taps on the Core Ball his holding and it begins to glow, activating so they can help her reach her destination.